BADR A

A NOVEL

Five Days Untold

TRANSLATED BY CHRISTIAAN JAMES

daab

Badr Ahmad

Five Days Untold (Novel)

Translated by: Christiaan James

© 2021 Dar Arab For Publishing and Translation LTD.
United Kingdom
60 Blakes Quay
Gas Works Road
RG3 1EN
Reading
United Kingdom
info@dararab.co.uk
www.dararab.co.uk

First Edition 2021
ISBN 978-1-78871-083-1

Copyrights © dararab 2021

دار عرب للنشر والترجمة
DAR ARAB FOR PUBLISHING & TRANSLATION

This is a work of fiction. Unless otherwise indicated, all the names, characters, businesses, places, events and incidents in this book are either the product of the author's imagination or used in a fictitious manner. Any resemblance to actual persons, living or dead, or actual events is purely coincidental.

The views and opinions expressed in this book are those of the author(s) and do not reflect or represent the opinions of the publisher.

Text Edited by: Marcia Lynx Qualey
Text Design by: Nasser Al Badri
Cover Design by: Hassan Almohtasib

"Be a coward my son! Be a coward! Nothing in this world is worth spilling your blood."

- Shifaa the Circassian (January 3, 2018)

Chapter 1

The Family of Muhi Al-Deen Al-Niqash

December 31, 2017

New Year's Eve

That day (on which it was said the number of cats and dogs surpassed the population) was an exceptional one in the history of my small town. Not because a year of war had come and gone while another was about to begin, but rather because peculiar events had taken place during that day. It wasn't the events themselves that were strange—any of which could have happened in any country in the world—rather, the curiousness lies in each event following in the wake of the other.

At seven o'clock in the morning, the town's men went to inspect the large tank that had been erected and placed on a high iron tower to the east of town, supplying it with water. When the men reached the tank, they found four decomposed and decapitated corpses in army uniforms bobbing on the surface of the green water.

Three days earlier, one of the workers in the Office of Sanitation, a widow, noticed that the water coming out of the tap in her kitchen was greenish and had a terrible smell. The imam of the mosque confirmed what the widow had said and added—spitting off to the side—that he had witnessed torn pieces of flesh flowing out of the house's tap. That same day, a violent wave of nausea and diarrhoea ripped through the town, causing the deaths of eight people. Once everyone had agreed that the water was the culprit, the imam suggested inspecting the tank of potable water. All the men in the village agreed.

The men kept their composure but were at a loss as to how they would pull the four bodies out of the tank. A new arrival to the town, a contractor in his forties, suggested getting a crane and hooking up the bodies to extract them. Everyone thought his plan was sound, but when they began to raise the first body, the metal chain tore it into several pieces. The stench of death and rotting flesh overwhelmed the area. The men of the village decided to leave the bodies in the tank and close it down for good after cutting the town off from the water entirely.

10 o'clock in the morning

Detachments from the army and police circled the small village. A number of homes were raided in search of alleged revolutionaries. Finally, the imam was arrested and led barefoot, blindfolded, and handcuffed to the town square. Able to hear but not see, he remained kneeling amid a crowd of military men, police, and those who were simply curious.

At some point, the imam of the mosque made out the voice of Naji Awad, an officer of the Political Guidance Committee. He overheard him talking to a captain in the army, demanding to take over the case from him. He shouted as the captain, caught off guard, couldn't find anything to say or do other than acquiesce to the wishes of an officer from Political Guidance, who without missing a beat led the mosque's imam to an unknown location.

The imam of the mosque was guilty of simply suggesting that the men check out the water tank. There were no revolutionaries in the town or even anyone who sympathized with the revolutionary rebel movement, nor had anyone hidden a criminal coming from outside the village. The authorities knew that, but the problem—the entire problem—rested in the fact that the tank was located within the territory of the town.

Noontime

The January sun dipped behind a large black cloud while the afternoon call to prayer was late by a full four minutes from its appointed time. Meanwhile, an upstanding young man saw the shop door of the metalworker Yahya Al-Rumi ajar, although it normally was closed at that time. The young man was a volunteer teacher in a school where all of the six classrooms were tents. He would often go around collecting donations for impoverished families and those who had been displaced by the war. He had an appointment with the metalworker to pick up twelve brass water taps, which he had donated to the town mosque.

The young man approached the door and pushed it open. Puzzled, he looked left and right, then slowly crept into the shop. He didn't notice the sound of large flies colliding against the glass of the shop windows, nor did he pay attention to the stench of coagulated blood that filled the area. After taking another step, he saw the metalworker, Yahya, slumped over one of the showroom tables, staring at the ceiling with frozen, petrified eyes. Blood covered his neck and body and everything around him. The young man was stunned. The blood in his veins froze. Catching a glimpse of a pinkish cluster hanging from the left side of the metalworker's abdomen, he recoiled, backing up half a step. The taste of flesh and blood swelled within him as the scene spun around him. Then, losing consciousness, he collapsed onto a pool of thickened blood.

***

That evening, as if in anticipation of some calamity, the unsettling sound of dogs barking compelled me to leave my bed. That day had certainly been a real red-letter day for catastrophes. I looked out my window and saw dogs circling an unfamiliar mongrel.

I left my room and made my way to the living room. Huddled around the television, we were watching a live broadcast of the New Year's Eve festivities. Before the clock struck midnight, the transmission was interrupted so that the toothless Minister of Defence could appear on the television screen in his army uniform. He stood behind a small mountain of coloured flowers and a wall of microphones. After a few holiday greetings and well wishes, he announced the suspension of all military exemptions that his Ministry had previously extended. Affected individuals were now required to quickly make their way to conscription divisions to complete the procedures for joining the army.

The toothless minister's announcement dropped on us like a cruel bomb, killing speech and our entire ability to think. In that instant, my mother dissolved into tears. My father looked around at all of us, and then set his cup of coffee on a brass tray. As he made his way toward his room, his joints cracked, and he mumbled something we couldn't quite make out while my three sisters huddled like frightened pigeons off in a corner. That night, after the news—or rather the "bomb"—fell on us, I realised that the day I was to depart home and make my way to the war was just around the corner. And nobody in the entire world could stop it from happening.

I dropped everything and went toward the window.

***

Years ago, in my twenties, I would linger by that window with its old wooden frame and use a small mirror to reflect sunlight onto the face of a beguiling girl who I fancied. But she abandoned the window, me, and our dreams and got married the first moment opportunity knocked on her door.

The groom was a merchant who had spent a period of his life in Indochina, traveling about the region selling spices and perfumes. Several years before his marriage, he was standing on his balcony overlooking a wide square in one of Delhi's suburbs, sipping tea his Indian maid had infused with heaps of jasmine. He was happily watching a boisterous Indian festival when a brightly ornamented elephant entered the festival area. Drums beat and young ladies danced while coloured powders were thrown in people's faces. At that moment—at the height of the festivities—his wooden balcony collapsed underneath him and he tumbled into the crowd. In the hospital, the doctors put a cast around his upper thigh and pelvis and inserted nails of pure gold into the bone of his left forearm. Each year and during every autumn, those nails caused him excruciating pain, making my crush complain to her mother that it was this pain that transformed him from a rational being to a madman lacking all self-control.

After having bought her father a prosthesis from the online retailer Ali Baba to compensate for his left hand, which had gotten cut off in ambiguous circumstances more than thirty years ago, the merchant of spices and perfumes whisked away his bride, along with his luggage, to Sri Lanka. The girl was gone for years, gradually fading from my mind, until one day I found myself feeling nothing at all for her. I no longer thought of her, except when standing in front of the window as I was doing now—or when I saw her father and his prosthetic hand—but even then, it was a shrivelled memory, devoid of either love or hate.

During the first years of the war, I happened to see her as she was leaving her family's home. She had become a frumpy woman, leaning heavily on her left leg as she walked, pulling behind her an ornery young boy with a red birthmark on the nape of his neck, his hair the colour of pure bronze. She glanced at me quickly, then got into a big American sedan and was gone.

***

As I went on watching the deserted street, which heaved with dreariness and haze, I saw two shadowy figures quickly cross the road. My mother was talking on the phone, the sound of a helicopter whirred in the darkness above, and a cold wind blew. I slipped into the depths of memories—memories that this little family had kept to itself for twenty-five years, remaining aloof from the commotion of the world and the vicissitudes of fate.

I will tell you the story from the beginning. Not from its beginning but from its roots, for pain and stories are like trees. They have roots that nourish and sustain them, granting them the power to endure and to last. I can't find a more suitable place to begin the story other than that which started it all, at least as it relates to me. This point is Muhi Al-Deen Al-Niqash, my father.

A man in his seventies, he was calm and gentle-hearted, and exemplary in every way. He always opted for quiet and peace of mind, even if the path to both was long and difficult. His nickname, Al-Niqash, or The Sculptor, didn't come from nowhere. Carving and sculpting plasterwork was the profession that he had inherited from his father, who in turn had learned it at the hand of a Persian sculptor named Ali Reza, who had come to this village during the banana boom, a time when living here was pleasant.

Ali Reza had bought a small shop, in the oldest part of the town, from a villager who used to sell tamarind fruit and cheese made from goat's milk. He then transformed it into a workshop to manufacture and sculpt plaster. Once people had gotten to know him—having probed deep into his very nature—they loved him and nicknamed him Abu Salman, in honour of the Prophet's companion, Salman the Persian.

The hand of God dropped my grandfather into the workshop of Abu Salman during that bitter time. Back then, my grandfather was on the cusp of youth. He learned the profession from him, soaking it up with a great patience that is seldom seen among youth today. After some time, Ali Reza died, leaving behind no relatives. My grandfather inherited the shop and the occupation and kept the name "Abu Salman's Workshop," which Ali Reza had written in his distinctive hand on the wooden door. My grandfather didn't consider changing it or covering it up, not even for a moment. He kept working in the shop and handled everything inside it with great care and delicacy, as if the owner were still alive, watching over him.

When old age set upon him, he prepared to pass the occupation and management of the workshop on to my father. Like my grandfather, my father had spent the bulk of his life in Abu Salman's little studio—mixing plaster and cutting glass and mother of pearl to form coloured ceilings, intricate paintings, and facades inlaid with stained glass. His trade bestowed him with an unending absorption and limitless equanimity and silence. It built within him a profound love of isolation, organization, and the coordination of everything around him. All of which added a spiritual Sufi dimension to what he produced. Spiritual essence and material substance combined to make his works even more beautiful and more perfect, leaving his imprint in every house and shop in the town and surrounding countryside.

Suddenly, and after more than a half-century of work, Chinese plasterwork began to invade the marketplace. When my father saw it for the first time in front of his shop atop the car of a young dealer, he turned it over in his hands and grudgingly showed his admiration. He then put it back, turned around, and left. He wouldn't allow this into his shop. When I asked him the reason, he said with the quietude of an artist-dreamer, all the while turning a Chinese plaster mould of unknown origins over in his hands: "When a craftsman makes his handiwork, he prepares the plaster and purifies it carefully. Kneading it with his hands, he mixes his own sweat into its substance. When he pours and sculpts it, he leaves behind an imprint of his skin and the light brush of his breath."

For a moment, he remained silent. Then, indicating the mould in his hand, he said: "Look, my son. When a craftsman loves what he has made, he bestows upon it a part of his soul, enhancing it. This one from China was manufactured by soulless machines that provide the plaster with nothing more than pressure and heat. For that reason, when you look at it with the eye of an expert, you feel it is frozen and dead, even if it is beautiful."

My father's fanciful words did not form the basis from which all sculptors worked. The market was flooded with cheap wares coming from China. When my father saw the keen interest in them to the detriment of his own profession—which put him under extreme pressure—he acquired several of those pieces and shut the door of his workshop, not budging from it for days. During these decisive days, he inspected the Chinese moulds with a magnifying glass. He then began to break them apart, pulverizing them and mixing them with chemical solutions to break down their structures. He disregarded my claims that the material coming from China wasn't actual gypsum. At the height of his exasperation, he shooed me out of the workshop and closed the door, returning to his work of inspecting the synthetic material.

Just as exhaustion began to whittle him down, a slump hit his profession, sending it hurtling toward the brink of extinction. After teaching me the fundamentals and secrets of his work over so many years, he now found it necessary to leave the workshop to me.

I introduced many new modifications and additions to the workshop—including Chinese plasterworks.

My father never returned to the workshop after he left it, but settled in at home, spending the majority of his time in the courtyard, sitting on his rattan chair underneath the barren grapevine. He didn't move an inch from his sitting area except to go to the mosque. Out of sheer boredom, and burdened with free time, he began tinkering with ancient electric devices that had no hope of ever being repaired. At the end of each attempt, he would fly off the handle and destroy the device with his hammer. His free time brought out aspects of his personality and nature that had always lurked under the surface, most importantly his complaints about everything.

During that period, we grew accustomed to hearing his angry shouts bellowing from beneath the grapevine as he smashed the devices. It had become a daily routine. One day, we didn't hear his yelling or demolishing. Instead, we saw him sitting on his chair staring at the ground, frozen. A profound silence had descended upon him. We didn't pay much attention to this bout of silence. We thought that he had simply become bored with his repair attempts, and that he was thinking about taking up another hobby.

That day, the sky opened up and it began to rain. My mother looked out through the door of our house and called to him several times. He remained immobile and silent. Immovable. Like a wax statue. Panicked, she went over and shook him. When she felt the light brush of his breath on the back of her hand, she carried him by his armpits toward the house. I returned home quickly and found him sitting in the family room, my mother and sisters huddled around him, trying to elicit even one word or movement, but with no success. I moved closer and shook him a few times. He looked like someone unable to either hear or see and was incapable even of blinking.

We didn't waste any time, nor did we give a thought to the downpour. We brought the car around and hauled him to a whole array of private clinics in a neighbouring city. The first doctor said that he wasn't suffering from anything and just needed to get some rest. All he did was give us ten sedatives. My mother remained sceptical, so we went to a second clinic, then a third, but they didn't offer up anything more than what the first doctor had said. At night, we made our way back home with my father. After evening prayers, my mother made him swallow one of the pills, in the hopes that he would sleep and wake up having cast off this silence and odd behaviour.

Early the next morning, my mother didn't find him in his bed and woke us up in a fright. We scoured the house without finding him; however, we did notice that the door to the house was ajar. We went out into the courtyard and were surprised to find him sitting on his chair under the grapevine, silent, lost in thought as he had been the day before.

An Armenian neighbour, who adored my mother and who, for the past ten years, had been very partial to her coffee, visited us one morning carrying a sack of Ethiopian coffee beans for my mother. She saw my father on his chair in that state and noticed he didn't respond to her greeting nor did he pay her any attention, as he normally did. My mother explained in detail about his condition and the neighbour gave her the name and address of a doctor (one of her uncles' sons) who had a clinic in the neighbouring town. She assured her that he was a first-rate doctor and wouldn't charge too much money. Sparing not a minute, we transported my father in a neighbour's car, crossing through numerous checkpoints and earthen barriers.

We arrived at that poverty-stricken and garbage-filled village only to discover that the address the Armenian neighbour had given us was either old or incorrect. We had wasted half the afternoon searching for the doctor's clinic in rundown neighbourhoods that had been built during the time of the cartel.

After enormous efforts, we tracked it down in a remote working-class quarter, home to bird sellers and porters. We made our way to the clinic. There was no sign on its walls to indicate what it was. The clinic was empty, lit only by a waning light that pierced through windows that were covered by stained and ragged curtains. The stench of tobacco and urine filled the air. We heard muffled voices and made our way to the doctor's office, where we found him sitting behind a filthy desk laden with things no doctor needed in his clinic.

He was smoking and playing chess. When he saw us, he smiled and set the chess game to the side and gestured for us to take a seat. We sat on an overstuffed sofa next to a large pile of magazines from the 1980s. He listened to us, then got up and examined my father, performing a number of tests. He informed us—while his molars crushed something hard—that my father was stricken with a case of muteness that affected his speech. We were alarmed, but he put our minds at ease, confirming that it was a psychiatric illness and not contagious. My mother asked about the reasons for the illness. Reflexively stroking his rough beard, he said: "The germ of the disease resides in the bowels of male flies that live in the Caribbean, and it transfers to humans when the flies bite them.

We told him that my father had never left the country his entire life. Ignoring us, he lit a cigarette, and added: "There is still no known treatment for this disease. But it's not as dangerous as you might expect. Basically, what the patient needs is your understanding of his illness."

That is all the awful doctor said, not adding a single word more nor giving us any medicine. Instead, he left us and went back to his chess game and smoking.

We carried my father back to the house. We tried to accept him as he was, with his illness and silence. As days passed, and after minute observation of his behaviour, we discovered that the disease had not entirely made off with his memory. He still recognised faces and places, dates and voices. His eyes flashed when he saw or heard something that he liked, and his face would cloud over when irritated, making us realise he was still coherent. These facial expressions mirrored his interior state, and we started to rely on them to determine his wants and needs. This tiresome method was the first we'd discovered to pierce the wall of silence and confusion that isolated him from the world around. The situation continued this way for some time, until eventually we got used to it. With time, we forgot entirely that he once spoke and filled the world with his racket and shouting.

When the war broke out in the middle of the first month, the first missiles struck the outskirts of the village. A huge explosion reverberated, breaking windows, blowing off doors, and splitting open joints in walls. At that moment, my father was sitting under his grapevine. As the explosion echoed, he screamed hysterically and his whole body trembled. He kept yelling, although without moving from his chair. This was the first time he had broken the wall of silence that encircled him. After that, he slowly began to interact with those around him. We were caught off-guard, as he came out of his dazed silence so unexpectedly. He began to tell us stories and to narrate events that nobody remembered—and, even more strangely—had never even heard about before. His narration was very precise—the precision of someone who had actually lived through those details.

One morning, we found him in his usual spot beneath the grapevine. Next to him was a pile of olive wood, and another from a lemon tree, and laying on his workbench were woodcarving tools. We had no idea how or where he had procured them. From morning onward, he carved geometric shapes, exotic faces, and strange masks into the wood. When he finished one, he stained it with olive oil and then placed it with the care of an artist into the oversized wooden armoire in the entryway of our house, all without seeking the family's thoughts or opinions.

It seemed as if, through this hobby, he had discovered his soul. Unlike previous times, he didn't give up and kept at it energetically and purposefully without even a pause. When the cabinets and floors brimmed with carvings, he began to line them up inside the house. We were surprised when we saw piles of high-quality wood beside him. We had no idea where he had gotten them. Then, unexpectedly, a bout of scurvy struck his body, and he suffered severely. His mouth and tongue swelled, and lesions appeared on various parts of his body. During that time, he was constantly shouting and complaining of the pain. We were shocked. We had never seen him suffer and shout in such a way and didn't know what was hurting him. On multiple occasions in the early days of his disease, my mother would invoke an incantation and prayed fervently to God on his behalf. His condition deteriorated and his suffering became more acute, so we took him to multiple doctors. Afterward, my mother began to take care of him exceptionally well and gave him his medicine on schedule and as much orange juice to drink and tamarind fruit as she possibly could. His condition slowly improved and, after thirteen months of suffering and losing most of his teeth, the disease finally left him.

True to her name, my mother, Shifaa, was a cure for the heart and soul. Well-spoken and deeply logical, she loved truth and clarity as much as she loved her Turkish coffee and Byzantine rugs. She seized each day and its events like a bull by the horns. She had a solution for every problem and an uplifting word for every dispiriting thought. In her chest, she carried a strong heart that neither her many years nor the eight cups of coffee she insisted on drinking every day, since the earliest days of her youth, had managed to exhaust. Her heart remained steadfast in the face of the world and its concerns and embraced us, making her the cornerstone of the household and our lives.

As for my father, his wholehearted devotion to his work kept him isolated from our problems and our lives, causing a strange emotional gap between us that you rarely find between father and child. He was a stranger to us and, in his eyes, we were irritating entities to be handled with a surly coarseness. Sometimes I attributed the reason for this gap to his isolation in his shop and his love for his work. Other times, I attributed it to my mother's behaviour as she laboured to lift the burden of the family and its problems off my father, which resulted in his isolation. I never found a rationale for this exhausting work other than her deep love for my father and her desire to distance him from anything that bothered or irritated him. She would not have done it had she not been strong and courageous, or if she'd lacked sufficient patience and wisdom to face the days and their vicissitudes.

I don't remember anyone ever breaking the strict rules she set in the house. These rules went beyond mere organizing of daily affairs. They determined where occupants of the house put their afternoon shoes, when and how they drank their tea, which direction soap in the bathroom was placed, and how you should stand when addressing someone. My father was not oblivious to any of this despite his isolation. I often heard him say that my mother should have been a town mayor or chief of police. Every time she overheard him say this, she smiled, holding the tips of her braids, and agreed:

– I can do it all, and you'll see—this one braid is equal to a thousand moustaches!

My father rarely called her by her name, but rather referred to her as "Bint al-Muthammar". As for the women in the neighbourhood, they called her the "Circassian", which made my mother very proud despite how strange it sounded to the ears of those who weren't in-the-know. She was extremely proud of her roots. Her father, Kemal Bek, was Circassian, and he had come with the Turks who accompanied a Turkish investment company working in the banana sector. Faced with the colossal strength and power of the banana cartel, this small company didn't last long, so he ended up selling his assets to one of the cartel's firms. And that's how my grandfather, Kemal Bek, was able to join the company as the executive director in one of its branch offices.

He chose his wife from one of the established families. In fact, life treated him so well that he wanted to stay on, even after the cartel had departed. Under the umbrella of protection from his wife's family, their influence and standing sponged away his past, just as it had wiped away the epithet "Kook" from his national identity card and provided him with a job at the Antiquities Council and then later in the Office of Agricultural Yields at the General Council for Export.

My mother, Bint al-Muthammar, had only one brother, who lived in the capital. His name was Ragheb, and he had never visited us; despite that, he called my mother daily, and they would talk for hours. These long calls caused my father to call him a "chatterbox" each time his name was brought up, and for many years he shunned talking to him. She made my uncle Ragheb privy to the details and secrets of our lives as if he were living with us to such a degree that he would ask whether one of our sisters had finished sewing something or if another sister had completed embroidering the hallway curtains. It didn't stop there, and he would offer his opinion on colours and styles each time he received photos via WhatsApp.

A secret about my mother that only we knew was that she was slightly hard of hearing, which affected her ability to hear sounds clearly but went unnoticed by others. She told us that she relied on reading lips. For that reason, it was no wonder that I would see her make her phone calls by video. These calls had a specific pattern that was seldom broken. When the phone would ring, she would take it to her favourite corner in the family room next to the window and set it up on a small table in front of her beside a cup of Turkish coffee. She would open the phone and speak to the caller in a loud voice while her facial expressions danced about and hands gesticulated, emphasizing this or refuting that, as if she were a well-seasoned lecturer and her interlocutor were a miserable pupil sitting nervously in a chair in front of her. Those who didn't know her secret misinterpreted this behaviour, but it was all the same to her. She didn't think for a moment of revealing her secret, even if it caused some people to keep their distance and label her as uppity. For her, appearing strong to others was preferable to seeming impotent and broken.

My three sisters—Hinaa, Nadaa, and the youngest, Ilham—were all younger than me, each separated by only a few years. My father notated the birth of each one on the inside cover of his large Quran. Hinaa was born the day the Pakistani president Mohammed Zia passed away, and Nadaa was born the same day Saddam invaded Kuwait, while Ilham was born the day the war in Yugoslavia ended, which happened to be the very same day phone lines came to our village.

All three of them were identical in looks, comportment, and dress. Down to their tastes and thoughts, they were totally in sync—something rarely seen, even among twins. I recall that they spent their placid childhood together, never apart, playing in the same spot without any deviation, and often we would find them sleeping on the same bed and under the very same blanket.

As they grew, so did their synchronicity, and we would watch them gallivant about the house and do their chores together as if connected by a hidden link. I don't remember ever hearing one of them argue with another. Rather, they showed deep interest in what each of them was doing, and they excelled at creatively making that apparent. It was as if they thought with one mind and saw with one eye. That total compatibility became their entire universe and made the outside world irrelevant. Naturally, they became antisocial, with a predilection toward isolation and seclusion. Even attending events or engaging with other people drove them crazy. This trait, my father would say, came from his mother and sisters, who never left the house except on rare occasions. It's no wonder that they spent the better part of their lives unknown in their own neighbourhood.

My sisters' inclination toward seclusion pushed them to stop their studies early, even before the eldest could correctly do dictation. They settled down happily at home and passed time by crocheting and making handicrafts. And so it was no surprise that our entire house inside started to look like a craft fair.

Chapter 2

Ziad Al-Niqash

My name is Ziad. Yet on happy occasions, my father calls me Abu Tariq. I was born on a day the world stopped in its tracks. My father jotted down the date of my birth on the inside cover of his large Quran without noting anything else, as he had done for my sisters. But the many drops of ink that fell from his pen next to the date betrayed that he had spent more than a short while thinking of the nature of the event that he would connect to my arrival into the world. After some time, and in a different pen, he added: Ziad was born two and a half months after the Chernobyl nuclear reactor exploded.

My birth was difficult, and my mother had to be transferred to the hospital. Before too long, she told us that an Irish nurse with freckled cheeks named Rebecca was the one who oversaw my birth. This often upset my father, who would say in a tone of someone who knew deep secrets that the person who birthed me was none other than a depressed American nurse named Dorothy, who was religious, lively, and beautiful. Yet she would inexplicably abandon her patients and go to the hospital bathroom to cry for hours on end.

Every time the story came up, the person who had helped my mother give birth remained a point of contention between my mother and father. I don't think that, after all these years, that either one of them conceded to the other's side of the story or would allow us to believe the other's version. One morning, after his bout with muteness was over, my father unexpectedly mentioned that nurse. He began calling for my mother from under his grapevine. We went and stood before him. With eyes glued to the ground and not moving a muscle, he asked my mother:

– Do you know why Dorothy was depressed and constantly cried?

For a few moments, he fell silent. We heard the raspy wheezing of his chest, which had calcified long ago from layers of plaster dust. Then, without lifting his eyes from the ground, he said:

– She carried a child in her womb after having gotten pregnant from a fling with a boy in his twenties whose brown skin had entranced her. When she informed her Catholic parents by mail, they told her to abort the foetus, and they gave her an ultimatum: either the baby or them.

This was a new dimension to the story that my father had added after more than three decades and while in a difficult psychological state. There was nothing, however, in this addition that decisively settled the debate (which had, in any case, persisted for decades) in favour of my father's telling. My mother just shook her head numbly without uttering a single word. And that is why the story of my birth remains as it is: Two stories told to satisfy two different sides.

Given that I was the only son that the Creator had willed for a family whose progeny was predominantly female, I ought to have been raised like a king. But that was not the case. Rather, my early childhood was spent like anyone else's. Nothing distinguished it or set it apart, except for my father's fearful dread of everything I did. This fear, which was rooted in an anxiety over the lurking unknown, ate away at him.

When the first signs of adolescence began to appear on my face, bilharzia struck me unexpectedly. My only weakness was my love of rain. From the dawn of my childhood, I loved going out and playing in it; however, bilharzia riddled my body and did a real number on my kidneys. Sparing no effort or expense, my father had every doctor examine me. Yet by the time the doctors cured the bilharzia, it had already stolen away my youth and vitality, its flame having been extinguished deep within my weak eyes. And my body, with its swollen veins and gaunt, bamboo-like stalks for limbs, had grown emaciated and sallow.

When I graduated high school, my father tossed my diploma off to the side and said to me:

– You've become a man, and you've got all the education you need. Now you have to master a skill that will serve you well throughout your life.

He was in his room reading his large Quran. His response was forceful and came out of the blue, which showed that he had planned it beforehand and had only been waiting for the right moment. It wasn't his response that irked me so much—it doesn't take a genius to realise that he was at an age when he needed to rest, and it was critical that I became the family's bread-winner. What bothered me about it was how he dealt with the issue with such sterility. I had thought that, when I succeeded in getting this diploma, I would be achieving a long-awaited dream of his and that I would receive praise and congratulations to such an extent that his feeble breath could hardly keep up.

I had nothing to say to him. Even if I had found something to say, a man like him was impossible to convince once his mind had been made up. I surrendered to his will and went to the workshop.

During my first days there, he instructed me in how to mix colours and make vegetable dyes. Every day, he offered me a new tidbit extracted from the depths of his knowledge. But I was a young man eager to embrace life and enjoy it to the fullest. I was not at all fond of the workshop or of being trapped within its four walls, isolated from the bustling world outside. When my emotions got the best of me and the intensity of adolescence boiled over, I got a small recording device to listen to the latest hits.

But because of his moody disposition, my father refused to let me listen to music. So I hid my prized possession behind some sacks of plaster and I longed for when he would leave so I could listen. Yet despite the recording device beside me, plaster sacks and panes of coloured glass continued to smother me.

I worked hard to ignore it all, to see it as a normal kind of life. But I failed. I couldn't stop watching my peers with envy. As the days passed, my world became the workshop, and I grew content with reality. And though it was truly a strain, I became accustomed to my prison, if also shy and dithering. I could not stand up for myself nor was I well-spoken, even if I were in the right. I started to fear people and avoided interacting with them as much as possible. On many occasions, I was unable to manage myself or my affairs well. How could I? I was a wretched prisoner trying to enjoy his imprisonment just so I could be happy!

Despite it all, my emotions continued to develop, and my imagination began to blossom. As time passed, I mastered my father's trade and began to compete with his creativity by imitating sculptures I found on the internet. But my father never once said: "Well done." Rather, he excelled at looking for mistakes—even making them up—just to give him a reason to berate me.

One evening, after a long period of isolation in the workshop, I sat in the living room of our house while my mother was talking on the phone with one of the neighbours. I heard our neighbour tell her about a dream she'd had. Her voice echoed into the living room, saying:

– I dreamed the hair on my head was falling out. Not strand by strand but fistfuls! Three tufts to be exact.

When I heard her words, as if reading an open book, I said:

– If she has a debt, she should pay it off within three days!

I uttered the words unconsciously, but my mother's ear did not miss them. After she finished her call, she asked me what I had said. I repeated that she should tell the neighbour she ought to pay off her debts within three days. My mother stared at me for a few seconds then took the phone and dialled the neighbour's number. When her voice answered on the other end, my mother said:

– Um Muhammed, I asked for an interpretation of your dream, and I was told that if you have a debt, you should pay it off within three days!

She paid her debts. Three days later, death stole away with our neighbour.

That evening, my mother informed us that her father, Kemal Bek, used to interpret dreams like no one else. His interpretations never missed their mark, even when he specified something down to the number. And he would describe specific things as if he were the one who had seen it himself.

Since then, visions and dreams piqued my interest. I relished interpreting and cracking their codes and my satisfaction soared when my interpretations proved to be spot on (which they were, except in rare instances). So I became a sort of destination for confused souls, the elderly, and those whose despair had flung them to the brink of delusion. This isn't to say that my lifestyle changed, rather the opposite. My father tightened the noose around me and my phone calls. He accused my mother of leading me down the path of evil and prevented me from receiving people and listening to their visions. As usual, I obeyed his wishes and plunged myself deeper into isolation. Dreams still came to me, though: surreptitiously, written on paper, and delivered by skilful messengers.

Chapter 3

Naji Awad

January 2, 2018

Naji Awad, an officer in the Political Guidance Committee, woke up early from his sleep to the ringing of his mobile. He stretched a hand toward the nightstand and grabbed it. Staring at it for a few seconds, he answered groggily:

– Yes...

– Good morning, sir

– Yes!

The voice on the other end was perplexed:

– I called, as you asked. So we could distribute the notices that—

Naji Awad cut him off:

– Yeah, yeah. What time is it now?

– Seven a.m.

He rubbed his face with a palm and said:

– I'm coming.

He closed the phone and tossed it on the nightstand, sending the bottles of aspirin and cologne flying. Fathiya, his wife, startled awake. She cast her tired gaze between him, the nightstand, and everything on the floor. Irritated, she stretched a hand out toward him and said, in exasperation:

– What's all that?!

He didn't turn toward her. He lit a cigarette and said, sharply:

– Go make me a cup of tea.

She turned to the other side, pulling the comforter over her body, and with clear annoyance, said:

– The kitchen is right in front of you, you feckless son of your father!

He didn't want to start the morning off with a fight, so he quickly dressed and left the house. Once in the street, he felt his side only to discover that he had forgotten his revolver. He turned around to go back. At that moment, the words of the first officer he had worked under drifted back to him. The man had told him, on a similar occasion, "Your weapon is your honour."

The phrase knocked around inside him. He let out a curse and opened the house door. Then, like a reckless officer on a night raid, he dashed toward his bedroom. He opened the nightstand drawer, scattering its contents, then shoved his hand under the pillow and took his gun. Slipping it into his holster, he turned around and began to walk out. But before he could cross the threshold, his wife awoke from her sleep and launched into a rage that was audible to the entire neighbourhood. Nobody paid much attention to her screams. They had gotten used to hearing fights between Naji Awad and his wife all the time. Night and day.

Shortly after, he was propped against the wall across from the mayor's house, accompanied by a gaunt-looking soldier. As he puffed on his cigarette, he continuously inspected the windows, while the soldier diligently knocked on the door every two minutes, trying to rouse the mayor despite the fact that he had already responded and asked for ten minutes to prepare his papers and get dressed. Naji Awad was cognizant of the fact that this old mayor had been able to do what he himself could not. Three weeks ago, he had married a young woman in her twenties who had been internally displaced by the war. Or perhaps more accurately, he had aced out Naji Awad for the heart of this young girl.

It was no surprise that he remained envious of him and laid in wait for an opportunity to score a hit on the mayor's young wife, who he had met during the early years of the war at the police station while setting down her name in the registry of Internally Displaced Persons. Back then, he insisted she unveil her face so he could check it against her identity card. Her beauty astonished him. From that moment on, he hadn't ceased fabricating reasons and waiting for opportunities to summon her or pay a call on her family.

Incidentally, she provided him with ample opportunities to make the intentions of his heart clear. She wanted a husband who could reunite her and her family, and she had no qualms associating with someone with the sort of chequered history that he had. But he didn't want a wife. Just a mistress to fool around and amuse himself with. Nothing more.

When this dawned on her, she slammed the door of opportunity in his face. He began to harass her family and terrify her sisters by threatening them with imprisonment on trumped-up charges. Still, the door to her heart remained shut. When she married the mayor—and he had no idea how that came to be or was even arranged—it curbed some of his desires. However, he couldn't distract himself entirely from thinking about her. For that reason, he had to keep getting in her way again and again. The mayor himself was unaware that Naji Awad was regularly setting obstacles for his wife and Naji Awad saw that as a clue as to why she didn't resist him. It never crossed his mind that this pitiful wife feared the harm that would befall her family if she stirred up trouble between him and her husband.

The mayor left his house in a hurry, carrying a large folder filled with stacks of paper under his arm. He greeted Naji Awad and the soldier, and then began leading the way. Naji Awad flicked his cigarette off to the side and followed.

He kept inspecting him closely from behind, examining his dry and worn-out skin. His knotted and calloused fingers. He tried to imagine what these fingers had touched the night before. In that moment, he imagined he'd caught the whiff of some captivating fragrance wafting up from the folds of the mayor's clothes and he immediately dove into a sea of never-ending numbness.

Standing in front of the first house, the mayor drew him back from his reverie. He knocked the door with his cane and called out to the owner in a loud voice. After reciting its contents by heart, he handed him one of the notices and then, returning the signed copy to the folder, he scrawled a note and closed it. Their visit to pre-selected houses in town followed one right after the other. Naji Awad stopped and, with an air of impatience, said:

– How many are left? We're tired!

The mayor pointed to the end of the road and, at that moment, he looked stronger than Naji Awad had expected. Then with a parched mouth, he said:

– Only one house left. The residence of Muhi Al-Deen Al-Niqash.

Naji Awad kept staring at his wrinkled face and crusty, chapped lips. He asked himself: I wonder if he kissed her with those?

Before he went too far with his questions and imagination, the mayor continued on his way, saying:

– Come on! Let's get this done.

After a few moments, both of them were standing at the gate of Muhi Al-Deen Al-Niqash. The mayor knocked on it with his cane, but there was no answer. They pushed the door open and crossed the courtyard toward the house's front door. The mayor rapped on it with his cane a second time and called out loudly for Muhi Al-Deen Al-Niqash, a hint of annoyance in his voice. Naji Awad whispered as his eyes scanned the house's courtyard:

– They say this man has lost his marbles.

Before the weary mayor could respond, the door opened. When he saw Al-Niqash standing before them, Naji Awad took two steps back. He wasn't crazy as had been said. He was a middle-aged man, neat and calm in appearance and demeanour, though with a trace of confusion across his face. He dismissed all this from his mind. He just wanted to finish the job and get out of there. In a flash, he saw a radiant face from inside the house. Seconds later, it submerged into the darkness, and all at once his entire being shook. He lost track of everyone around him but managed to snap back upon hearing the mayor say:

– We're done here.

He recovered himself and, a bit confused, said:

– Really? Let's go!

The two of them traversed the town's streets, heading toward the police station to turn in the signed notifications. Naji Awad didn't like to ride in cars (due to a story we will mention later) and only did this if forced. As for the tired mayor, he finished his task on foot despite the fact that walking great distances wore him out completely. He had no other option and didn't want to run the risk that someone might think he was derelict in his duties.

He also knew full well that Naji Awad would not have his back or protect him at all during their walk. It was as if he were sedated: he saw and heard nothing. All at once, the mayor cried out from pain in his left knee. Naji Awad awoke from his daydreaming and cursed the mayor deep within his heart. He also cursed the young wife who at that very moment had become hideous to him, her rejection making him hate her even more.

***

That evening, he was the first to arrive at the nightly gathering spot, where he and his circle of friends had the habit of spending their evenings drinking and playing poker, left unperturbed by anyone's questions or eyes. Fittingly, the gathering took place in a secluded hovel that overlooked the cemetery on the east side of town. It was owned by an old man beset by bad luck, whose once-vast fortune had disappeared except for that room and the paltry rent it generated.

Naji Awad ate his dinner and then tucked himself into a corner, smoking and drinking tea while chatting away on his phone. At nine o'clock, his evening pals began to arrive one by one. The table, which in another life had been used for billiards, filled with cards, glasses, flasks, money, and ashtrays. And as the air thickened with smoke and body odour, the place grew louder and more boisterous, filled with Naji Awad and his companions.

The group broke up before three in the morning, leaving Naji Awad alone at the table, his mind empty, staring at nothing. Suddenly and unexpectedly, the angelic face that he had seen at the Al-Niqash residence flashed before him, flickering inside him and arresting his ability to think. He couldn't understand how he could have forgotten about it after leaving the house, and he didn't know why he remembered it now.

However, one of his companions stepped into the room and pulled him out of his reverie. Antar greeted him and placed a large container on the table. He sat down and opened it up. The smell of grilled fish filled the place. He disappeared outside for a few moments, then returned carrying three green flasks. Seated again at the table, he ripped off a big chunk and shoved it into his mouth, saying:

– Alright, then. *Bismillah*.

Naji Awad stared at him for a few seconds before he limply stretched out a hand and began chewing with little appetite. Antar noticed that he was not himself and set aside his bite, saying:

– What's wrong with you today?

It was the first time in his life that Naji Awad felt something was wearing him down. He stopped eating, rested his back against the wall, and lit a cigarette. His interest piqued, he asked:

– What do you know about the Al-Niqash family?

Antar was an assistant in the secret police. He placed a bite in his mouth, filling it completely, then asked:

– A security issue? Or...?

Cutting him off with a wink, Naji Awad wiped his hands together and said:

–No, it's not security related.

Antar let out a guffaw while Naji Awad shook his head, adding:

– It's not what you think.

Antar didn't believe him. He didn't believe the issue was security-related, and he decided to keep pressing. Antar's only interest lay in what could benefit him personally. Naji Awad's caprices had no end, and there was no predicting his desires. He had often relied on Antar to make his "missions" successful, as Antar would undertake whatever was entrusted to him to the fullest. In return, Naji Awad was not at all stingy toward him and treated him with a great deal of care and affection.

Antar opened one of the flasks, gulped down as much as he could, then let out a belch and stared at Naji Awad, who at that moment looked depressed and despondent. He sensed that this time the issue was different. With rare sincerity, he asked:

– Naji, what do you want to know about them?

Naji Awad mindlessly stroked his Saddam-esque moustache and cast his gaze through the window, into the darkness. He said:

– Everything, everything!

Antar was engrossed in chewing, swallowing, and drinking. His interest now aroused, he stopped and suddenly asked:

– What ever happened to the imam of the mosque?

Naji Awad stared at him from behind a cloud of smoke without saying a word. He snuffed out his cigarette and weakly flicked his finger intimating he had gone away, flown off. Been dealt with. Then he went back to staring at nothing.

But don't let the despondency cloaking the face of Political Officer Naji Awad fool you. It could be just a temporary disturbance or a mask. No one on the face of this earth believed him, even when he was being honest. As for his employment at the police station, he had never before worked as a political officer. However, he shoved his nose into everything around him and performed whichever aspects of the work that best suited his interests and whims, doing so with a remorseless selfishness that had no match. That's why they called him the "Executioner." Not merely the executioner of the police station, or of the town, but of the Ministry of the Interior itself!

This epithet didn't bother him. He was rather pleased by it, in fact, even though nobody dared say it in his presence. In his mind, the nickname had developed out of people's fear of him—the result of gossip and wagging tongues—and reflected the extent to which terror had gripped their hearts.

Don't be surprised, either, if I were to tell you that he was fully aware that everyone—his friends, his enemies, and those who could be both—all knew that he had killed a fishmonger a few years back in a neighbouring village and chucked his body into a broken refrigerator. Nobody discovered the body before it had completely decomposed. Likewise, they knew that he was the one who had stabbed a prostitute with a screwdriver below the chin, and that she would have bled out in the middle of the road had it not been for a passerby who took her to a hospital. Lying on her bed like a discarded plank of wood, the prostitute managed to cling to life, but was unable to speak or move. When one of the detectives informed her that some human rights activists had come to coax her into filing a lawsuit against him, he paid her a visit late one Thursday night. He broke the lock at her house, assaulted the servant, and when the incapacitated prostitute saw him approach, her whole being quaked, and she let out a panicked cry. But he couldn't give a damn. He sat beside her bed and stared into her terrified face for several seconds. Then suddenly, his expression tightened, and he spat in her face. Her facial muscles contracted, and her mouth went dry. Grabbing a pillow, Naji Awad proceeded to smother the life out of her. He left the house after cutting off the breasts of the servant with a razor blade, threatening to slit her throat if she said a word about what had happened.

He also was aware that they knew how, during the early years of the war, he had spelled out the words "traitor" and "rat" in gunpowder on the chests of some captives and then set it on fire.

As the ferocity of the war intensified, many taboos and red lines dissolved. One moonlit evening, he impaled three criminals in the town cemetery on a barren hill. That night, villagers heard screams of pain and panic, the likes of which they had never heard before.

During the war years, he used to manipulate the registry of those entitled to government assistance. He would add and delete, stop and prevent, barter, sell, and buy. When he noticed the disgust and indignation on the faces of the international aid workers, he would cite "security reasons" and assured them that "orders from on high" formed the basis of his actions.

These justifications never fooled anyone, so he had to rule with a heavy hand. He would imprison the aid workers, assault them in the depths of the night, and set their cars ablaze. When one of the branch directors of an aid agency complained to the authorities in the capital, he torched the branch's storehouses, foodstuffs and all. Afterward, the branch withdrew its complaint and moved on.

Between this thing and that thing, everyone obeyed and submitted to him without debate. In fact, Naji Awad didn't care what people knew or didn't know. He didn't give a damn. The only thing that occupied his mind was asserting his authority and controlling everyone around him. He even managed to co-opt the chief of the police station, the representative from the intelligence services, and the officer in the mobilization division. His word was supreme, and his interests were the ones most worth preserving. When faced with an obstacle, he did not hesitate to apply his golden rule: "What does not come easily will come by force."

His total confidence in himself and his conviction in his right to do as he pleased created within some people a feeling or awareness that he didn't work alone. There were others providing protection and cover for him.

This situation reached its peak in the second year of the war, when he raided the Catholic patriarchate in one of the neighbouring villages under the pretence of looking for armed men and weapons. He didn't terminate this operation until he had emptied the patriarchate treasury of all its contents. Then he left. People expected this raid would be the straw that broke the wretched camel's back. The authorities would have to rein him in. But nothing of the like happened. Two weeks after plundering the treasury, he arrested and imprisoned a nun who was working in a Greek convent school. He released her two days later without providing a single reason for her arbitrary incarceration. The nun had no other choice but to depart to an unknown destination. The young students simply said she had transferred to the capital.

Chapter 4

The Family of Muhi Al-Deen Al-Niqash

January 2

My father had just finished the afternoon prayer and was sitting on his rug, muttering quietly to himself, when we heard several knocks at the door. It was the mayor calling out for my father in a booming voice that nobody in the village could mistake. At that moment, my heart sank to the floor and my mother's face went pale. My sisters began to whisper. Suddenly, and in a rare moment, my father awoke to his senses. He shot us a glance, then folded up his rug and scurried off to his room. He came back and opened the door. We peered at the tired face of the town mayor looking back at us. Next to him was the political officer, a scrawny soldier, and a swarm of curious children. My father stared at the faces as a hint of a smile flickered across his face. The mayor looked back at us with his dark, squinting eyes before mumbling a few words that were difficult to hear. Then, in a gravelly voice, he recited the text of the notice from memory:

– It is required to appear at the soldier conscription site on January 3...

He finished rattling off the text and then added my name—written in poor, shaky penmanship with a blue pen that dribbled more ink than necessary—scratching it onto a copy of the notice that had been xeroxed on an ancient machine.

My father listened to what the mayor had come to say and, as he did, his smile grew increasingly steadier. And like a cardsharp, he kept his winning hand to himself until the last moment. With considerable confidence, he pulled out the original exemption document that he had kept safe inside the large Quran in his room for years. Neither the mayor, nor the officer, nor even the curious children bothered to take a look. Instead, the mayor repeated the notice, and we heard the exact same words that we had during the Minister of Defence's speech, and which I had already explained to my father two days before.

With a trembling hand, my father slid the exemption document back into the pocket of his robe and patted it absentmindedly. Having accepted defeat, he signed the notification, then turned around and went off. I took a copy of the notice from the mayor's shaky hand and closed the door. Consumed by a mountain of fear and sadness, my mother's face peered back at me while my sisters, crying, gathered around, trying to offer me some comfort.

At the dinner table that evening, my mother remained silent, her head bowed, totally lost in thought. She tore the loaf of bread in front of her but didn't lift a morsel to her mouth. Her eyes, nose, and drooping voice all betrayed the fact that she had spent long hours crying and doing nothing else. My sisters ate their meal despondently—their eyes fluctuated between anxiety and fear as they darted around, avoiding each other's gazes. As for my father, he hadn't come out of his room since signing the notice.

I got up from the table and went to sit cross-legged in one of the corners of the living room beside the wooden trunk, where we preserved everything meaningful to the family. I opened the lid. Helplessness and worry washed over me. I began looking for nothing in particular and, in reality, was just trying to hide my impotence and weakness from those already crushed by sorrow on my account.

As for me, I wasn't scared of the war. Although how could I not be? I had seen it on the faces of those close to me and heard its thunderous footsteps mixed with the groans of the injured and the wailing of bereaved mothers who had lost their sons. Not infrequently, our town received throngs of refugees, the disabled, and widows despite it too being targeted by shelling on quite a few occasions. Regardless, my lack of fear sprung from my belief in destiny and my awareness that the war could offer the benefit of a quick death. However, I did find myself asking: How will I live in the trenches and bunkers? How will I fight? And how will I avoid being killed? I was unable to process it all. I wasn't made for this. I was created to draw and sculpt, to cultivate beauty in small corners, and to plant delight in people's souls. I couldn't imagine myself part of this free-for-all carnival of death. And I had no idea where fate was taking me and what awaited me in the end.

I spent a large part of the night preparing my backpack. When I was done, I threw myself onto my bed and stared at the ceiling. At some point, I got up and stood in front of the window. I gazed upon the houses in the town and saw them withdrawn and dark, beset with pain and sadness, and veiled in the sighs and anguish of widows and orphans. Off in the distance, explosions reverberated and windowpanes shook. At that moment, the millstone of war was elsewhere, grinding down this land that had been consumed by the spilling of blood since the dawn of history. No sooner would one war end than another would begin. An absurd matryoshka doll of wars and crises.

***

This war hadn't come out of the blue. Rather, it had sprung from a war that had raged in the country 120 years before. Historians called it the "War of Fingers." Its first seeds had been planted when banana companies came to the country from all around the world. Our country, the "country of bananas", was draped back then in poverty and isolation, despite its plentiful resources and the fertility of its soil.

Companies began competing to invest in the banana sector, and they cultivated every inch they could, digging wells and building irrigation canals to link the great rivers to far-flung corners of the country. They erected railways and airports and rehabilitated three harbours to welcome large steamers that transported gigantic shipments of bananas to the rest of the world. In the beginning, these companies jockeyed only amongst themselves, but soon the weakness of the political regime combined with the companies' ambition to take over the country entirely. In the end, they united to form a cartel which began to manage the country and to control what was left of its political decision-making.

Goods and cash flowed into the country, and living conditions improved a great deal. The farmer who had once been mired in poverty and ignorance was surprised by the boom and by the vast number of products that poured in. Streets and towns filled with newcomers who had arrived, bringing much along with them. During that period, people saw a gramophone for the first time in their lives and that device created a wave of shock, amazement, and fear among the people. The newcomers didn't cease to amaze the people, as they illuminated the streets with electric lamps and opened a number of movie theatres that showed two weekly films. Beyond that, they opened photo studios, while in the cities and countryside telegraphs clickety-clacked and radios emitted the staticky sounds of programs broadcast around the clock in five languages. Everywhere, restaurants served meals and drinks according to European recipes while bars and dance clubs opened up, and the people began to see luxurious parties held every Sunday by employees of the banana firms.

People left their old jobs behind and went to work for the banana companies. They did all sorts of jobs and began to only care about cash, goods, and wandering around the markets. With the arrival of a Russian bolshevist on board a steamer carrying cotton, vodka, and caviar, the first union movement began to take shape and quickly grew among workers, becoming a thorn in the cartel's side as it tried every which way to stop its growth.

In the end, they found no solution except for pulling the rug out from under the feet of the local workers and substituting labourers who were far more loyal and a lot less demanding. The cartel began to import and resettle workers they had brought from Asia and Africa, and gigantic cargo ships dropped them off at the country's ports, along with their lice and bedbugs. They had suffered greatly from starvation and indigence and were ready to do anything in exchange for food and shelter. They worked tirelessly on the banana plantations for pennies. Moreover, they were indebted and showed complete loyalty to the cartel. In terms of production and allegiance, the results were astonishing. Most importantly, it crushed the local syndicalist movement and forced the local workers to accept the lowest of wages.

The flow of foreign labour to the country continued unchecked and, after only five years, the local worker found himself sidelined entirely. Under the best circumstances, he found himself on a cattle farm or in a sesame-oil factory while the foreign workers monopolized the greater share of employment opportunities provided by the banana companies.

The local unions attempted to negotiate with the government to improve their working conditions, and a memorandum of understanding was signed, guaranteeing the integration of the local workforce into the banana factories, where they would receive a salary commensurate with the nature of the jobs, in addition to stopping the flow of foreign workers.

The cartel didn't comment publicly on the agreement, but its response came just eighteen days later. Workers at the three major ports awoke to the sound of the engines of huge ships bearing the hundreds and thousands of labourers the cartel had collected from various parts of the world, with their families in tow. As a result, riots and confrontations broke out between local workers and newcomers and the cartel used its workforce as a kind of army to crush the uprisings and commit atrocities, such as setting fire to houses and laying waste to the fields.

After forty days of this slaughter, England sent an envoy, Sir Richard George, to meet with heads of the cartel and try to convince them to lean toward peace and end the tensions. He succeeded to some degree, and calm returned once again to the banana republic, even though the agreement was solely between the British envoy and the cartel, with not even the slightest representation by the union movement or government. The president's office didn't comment on the events or the visit of the British envoy. In any case, it was said that the president had passed away eight years earlier, and the cartel had kept his death a secret in order to maintain control of the country.

Following that fragmentary agreement, the people of the banana republic were treated in a humiliating manner, and their possessions were seized by the newcomers. They had become a people without rights or possessions, and they had no other choice but to accept and submit to the catastrophes they faced.

And years passed...

The cartel swallowed up the republic wholesale. It built an army on the remnants of the state's weak military and increased pressure on the local population. One Sunday morning in April, the cartel's workers were surprised by the absence of their foreign managers. In the afternoon, they discovered that their families had also disappeared. Before sunset, everyone living in the banana republic came to the realization that the cartel bosses had fled the country in secret, due to the outbreak of war on the high seas.

Chaos flooded the banana republic. The newly arrived cartel workers left everything behind, leaving by ship and by plane and even by small boat and hot air balloon. Clothing and baggage were scattered along the roads leading to the harbours and airports. Some even set fire to their homes before leaving. At the docks, those departing thronged together, having rid themselves of what they didn't need, and they began to fight and kill one another in order to gain a place on a departing boat. It looked like a scene from the Day of Resurrection. Like an escape from certain death. Even the cartel army, equipped with the most modern weapons, dropped everything and hightailed it out of there like everyone else. Within three weeks, the majority of foreign workers had left. All that remained were a few stray pockets of men, the elderly, and widows and children.

The local population, who had concealed themselves within a secret leftist organization called the Movement of the Free Nationalists, seized the cartel army's weapons. With guns in hand, they exacted brutal and merciless revenge on the last remaining workers, burning their property and executing them in the town squares. Those who survived had their fingers and feet cut off, ensuring they were unable to work, forcing them to live off the charity that the nationalist government deigned to provide.

One historian recounts that the Free Nationalists loaded up a small truck with the fingers of those in the cartel who had survived and transported the cargo onto fishing boats at sea. They then dumped them at a point two nautical miles away from the area where they had disposed of the corpses of those they had killed. They then uprooted every banana tree and set them alight. After two months had passed, the banana republic was completely devoid of both banana trees and cartel. All that remained within its borders were weak, powerless minorities living in far-flung corners of the country. The Nationalists gave these minorities the name "Al-Kook," short for the word "cocktail," a reference to the jumble of their ethnicities and nationalities. That epithet later began to signify a person unable to take care of himself, one who waited around for handouts.

Fifty years after this war—known as the War of Fingers—those pockets of "Al-Kook" had become villages and cities stretching out for miles. Dozens had become thousands, and thousands became millions. The banana republic began growing and selling everything—except bananas. The post-war generations inherited the laws enacted by their forefathers, which ensured both the criminalization of cultivating and selling bananas and the second-class status of Al-Kook. However, the vast majority of those subsequent generations didn't know the truth about what had happened and had never even heard of the so-called War of Fingers.

Then, only five years ago…

In the land of bananas, protests broke out demanding justice and equality. Without exception, every group of downtrodden people took part. The demands were general and fair, and the protests rocked the fragile government. They also revived secret organizations that had previously been on life support, renewing their hopes for power.

Two weeks after the protests began, ethnicity-based and racist organizations connected to Al-Kook percolated up to the surface. Nobody had even heard of them except in tales told by the mentally ill living in caves and under bridges, or they had read about them in pamphlets strewn about the city streets in the early mornings of the first of October each year. These organizations soon unified and formed what began to be called the Revolutionary Liberation Movement, adopting the struggle to raise up the dispossessed and throw off the wrongs inflicted upon Al-Kook.

Most people denounced the movement's calls. The level of racism in the country had not yet reached a point that required armed revolution or waves of protests. Many of the restraints or prohibitions that had beleaguered the Al-Kook had already fallen by the wayside with the passing of years, and nobody remembered any longer what had taken place or why this nickname had been given to such a wide swath of people. However, the political leaders on both sides *did* remember and took advantage of every opportunity to rehash these events and bring them to the forefront of the people's minds in order to stoke hate.

There were those who listened and obeyed these calls, but the vast majority of people didn't believe there had ever been a conflict called the War of Fingers and believed instead that politicians and their ilk were simply dredging up old yarns told by grandmothers and those nearing retirement. They believed, in fact, that Al-Kook was nothing more than the name of an ancient forefather who had, in the remote past, migrated from the island of Sicily. Crossing oceans in a papyrus boat with his twenty sons and women he had gathered from all around the world, he settled in this country and was given the name Al-Kook. Some said that his boat was still preserved in the Natural History Museum next to his fearsome lance, some tufts of his hair, and the sole of his shoe, which was made from the skin of a deer. As for the cartel, it was nothing more than a malevolent Phoenician god with the head of a dragon, body of a human, and limbs of a cricket. Ancient murals that historians had found in the remote southern reaches of the country gave evidence for it, and even now witches write its name on their talismans.

Still, the authorities confronted these protests with oppression and ruthless barbarity. By the third week, the protests and strikes transformed into an armed rebellion led by the Revolutionary Liberation Movement, which had set itself up as the mouthpiece for Al-Kook. The political authorities said that a new cartel was funding the rebellion, in the hopes of returning to the banana republic. The Movement countered that they wanted nothing more than a dignified life and equal citizenship.

As days went by, the average citizen forgot the reasons why the war had broken out in the first place and simply clung to life, searching for some meaning. As for those who *did* remember, they did not believe that the interminable war was being fuelled by myths and totems alone.

The war bore down on us like a boulder, with all its terrible weight. Each morning gave rise to a never-ending sequence of destruction: Fractures, grave jagged wounds, and death. Anaemia festered inside bodies. One grave gave birth to another, and blood spilled copiously as cries of pain and loss echoed all around. There were orphans, widows, the disabled, and the homeless, clad only by the sky and cloaked in dirt and garbage. There were students who left their schooling to take up weapons. Walls defaced with posters and slogans. Destroyed buildings. Panicked eyes and dried lips. Endless processions of funerals. Jets assaulting the sky. Cholera. Stray bullets. Lines everywhere and pain in every corner, in every house. There was acrid smoke polluting the sky and ash filling chests. Mountains of rubble and wreckage.

In the first days of the war, people were fully confident that it would not last more than two weeks, and that it was nothing more than politicians' manoeuvres to score a few gains. Others said it was a game of wait-and-see between the Free Nationalists and the Revolutionary Liberation Movement. For that reason, people didn't take anything seriously.

Days passed much as they had prior to the outbreak, undisturbed by even the slightest change. The enmity that politicians had tried so hard to provoke failed to sow division among the people, the vast majority of whom stopped going off to war. However, when war resources were on the verge of drying up, the two sides raced to conscript people by force, to supply the frontlines with fresh blood. Nobody dared oppose them. The accusation of treason was all too readily applied to whomever ran away from military service. And the president had deputized military courts to handle civil cases, following the dismissal of the legislative council which had previously been headed by an advisor from the Al-Kook (at least according to the nationalists' telling), and which subsequently ordered all traitors to the killing fields after a single court hearing. The corpses of the condemned were buried in disgraceful pits established by the Free Nationalists during the first years of the war. These pits were located on the outskirts, where all manner of things befitting the name were dumped: from slaughterhouse waste to the sludge from the water tanks' sewage.

In the midst of all that terrifying insanity, there was a simple way to escape from both the war and legal prosecution: obtaining an exemption document from military service. Although it was nearly impossible, we knocked on every door and bitterly pursued it for months until a soldier led us to a middleman in the Ministry of Defence who was able to produce an exemption document in just one week, after receiving $400 US dollars and a chrome-plated Tokarev handgun.

After turning their noses up at humanitarian assistance centres during the initial years of the war, by the third year, people got used to standing at their doorsteps. In the middle of the fourth year, an elderly man cried out in front of the gate of one of these centres:

– People have become like cruel wolves! They have become like cruel wolves!

This elderly man experienced the first instance, in our town, of someone's government food rations vanishing. Months later, however, people got used to seeing men and women shouting where the older man had first cried out.

Halfway through the fourth year, the arrival of coffins slowed to a trickle and wasn't as nonstop as during the first three. This wasn't because the war had stopped. No, not at all. In fact, the war's tempo had increased, as it became even more ferocious. One of the gravediggers whispered in the ear of a colleague, pointing toward the cemetery chock full of coloured tombstones:

– All the men and teen boys have disappeared. Pretty soon there will be no one left in town except us!

His colleague smiled a jaundiced smile and added, hoarsely:

– And cats and dogs!

Nobody doubted it. The fourth year was cruel and bitter. Our days tasted like dirt and our dreams transformed into ash scattered about by a malevolent wind—without direction or place to rest.

Not infrequently, decent people were reduced to eating the leaves of trees as a substitute for scarce food, while the lower classes resorted to stealing and burglary. As for merchants, they began to falsify expiration dates and sold us everything, even if it had gone bad, from medicine to children's candy! Can you imagine grey-tinged milk? Its smell was like the stench of vomit. Or toothpaste that tasted like plaster, and medicine as thick as cream? Or flour that tasted of cinders?

Four years on, the war had turned everything in this country to dust. Were all our values bullshit? Four years had passed, leaving those who had survived as shadows, bewildered and dejected, content with starvation, sickness, and death. We experienced a contentment born of having grown numb to the catastrophes and famine brought on by the war.

Confronted with everything, there was nothing for us to do as we welcomed the fifth year, apart from ignoring all the catastrophes that currently beset us. We continued to hold on in the hopes that the wheel of life would somehow turn and bring us something more beautiful.

Chapter 5

Ziad Al-Niqash

January 3

The first day

I opened my eyes just as the muezzin intoned "Prayer is better than sleep" and made my way over to the mosque, passing through the empty streets and filling my chest with the cold, apple-scented air as I went. There, among a crowd of older men, I performed my prayers and gazed across at all the faces and corners of the room. This could be the last time I saw them.

When I returned to the house, I overheard my mother mumbling her morning recitations as I headed to my room to cinch up my bag. My mother and father were seated in one of the alcoves of the family room—both silent and despondent. The coffee and the dates in front of them remained untouched while their pale faces betrayed that neither had slept a wink the night before.

My mother stood up, trying to appear strong, and gave a faint smile. She hugged me, went to another room, then came back only to disappear once more. When she returned, she pushed a bundle of papers into my bag and avoided looking me in the eye. Through it all though, I could see a violent storm of tears had gathered in the far corners of her eyes, choking her words and stifling her breath.

My father remained seated—frozen—staring at the ground with tear-filled eyes. No sign of life appeared in him other than his trembling hands. Yet deep inside he was smouldering and torn to pieces, silently weeping and shouting, trying in vain to breach the walls of this disease that had surrounded his soul and snuffed out all his words. I hear you, Dad. I feel you. Like you, I am gutted and consumed by fire as I leave you like this. But what choice do I have? If only fate were in our hands.

I finished everything quickly. I didn't want to linger and prolong their suffering. All I could hope for was to leave this moment in their minds as sterile and devoid of feeling as I could. Maybe the feeling that I would be alright would grant them some consolation. But then again, maybe it would give them the false impression that I didn't care that I was leaving them at all. I gave them a long embrace and filled my whole soul with their smell. My mother cupped my face with the palms of her hands and then, with tear-laden words wrested from the depths of her heart, said: "If you hear the sound of bullets, protect yourself any way you can. And avoid the night and open spaces!" I couldn't respond. I nodded. As crying and pleading filled her voice, she added, "Be a coward, my son! Be a coward! Nothing in this world is worth spilling your blood!"

Tears fell from my eyes as I pulled her against my chest. I then hugged my three sisters while they sobbed loudly. I couldn't calm their fears.

A violent, hidden hand tore me away and pushed me outside, and I departed.

Yes, I departed. Behind me, I could hear dozens of doors creaking open, then shut. I heard skittish pigeons flapping their wings in the sky above our courtyard and my father clearing his throat while my mother sobbed. I quickened my pace. The town's cold streets appeared strange and deserted like never before, empty except for a handful of stray cats, a few passers-by carrying mountains of worry on their backs, and wearied widows, whose bodies had long since been gnawed away by sadness, balancing bundles of bread from Al-Khairy Bakery atop their heads. I didn't stop. Not even for a moment. I kept up my pace as I walked toward the Teacher's Institute. From there, I would be able to find a car to take me to the railway station.

I wasn't the first to arrive. The place was already teeming with people, thirteen of whom had been summoned for conscription. I found myself amidst a large commotion of sorrow. Eyes were puffy. Crying choked off words. And throats were filled with lumps. Those who were departing embraced their loved ones with warm, unbreakable hugs while shouts and sighs filled the air with a melancholy that made you realise nothing would ever be alright again. Sacks and bags exchanged hands. Girlfriends chose to cry alone behind half-opened doors and windows while others were bolder and approached, hiding behind tree trunks to say their goodbyes causing the travellers to join them in crying.

I looked around and felt dizzy. Strangled. I quickened my steps. And as I did, I crashed into faces and bodies, tears and luggage and prayers. I walked out into a clearing, leaving behind all that pain. I had to get farther and farther away. The whole situation hurt me profoundly, like a terrible dagger had penetrated the depths of my heart.

After about three hundred metres, I stopped beside a row of apricot trees. White blossoms showered down all around. An ancient taxi pulled up, and the middle-aged driver stared at me. I pointed off into the distance and asked him in a loud voice, "Railway station?"

Without responding, he shot me a look, then inched toward the door handle. The door opened with a funerary slowness as a faint wind began to pick up. Before I got into the passenger seat, I cast a long, teary look back at the carnival of sobs and sadness and toward the houses heaped one upon another like tattered matchboxes.

The driver turned the radio on and then took off down the road. It was as if he wanted to tell me: I'm not looking to chitchat, my boy, and I don't care who you are, and I don't care if you know how I spent my long-gone youth! You be quiet and I will, too. That will be best for both of us.

Half an hour later, the car came to a stop in front of the rail station. I paid the driver the fare then crossed a wall made of rock-filled barrels and another made of sandbags. Concealed behind it was a broken-down battery of SAM-7 missiles supposedly there to protect the skies above the station. I saw shark-nosed missiles with photos of deceased soldiers stuck to them. Scrawled onto the fins were the names of those who had passed by or dared approach. Underneath the time-worn and paint-chipped weapon, there was a mentally disturbed man wallowing in his own filth beside a sack of garbage and a dead puppy. A breeze began to blow, carrying with it the smell of diesel, grease, and engine oil.

On the opposite platform was the train that had arrived the previous night. Alongside it were fourteen wooden coffins. Four soldiers from the Protocol Office were draping them with flags.

The train station was filling up slowly with travellers, and I quickened my pace over the wet asphalt. Shoe shiners, porters, vagrants, cigarette sellers, beggars, and soldiers were everywhere. It was as if there had been no night and no sleep at all. Faces drifted by as I stood in front of the ticket window for five minutes. Then I made my way toward the 8 o'clock train just as it let out its first whistle.

On the platform were families, while in the windows sat the travellers. This man was waving, that woman was crying, while another gave advice, and a mother prayed as an infant cried. Sellers beckoned toward their wares and beggars placed their hands on your chest, tugging at the hem of your clothes. The stench of their breath and body odour. Pungent perfumes and fragrant plants. I heaved my body through all this and made my way toward the train. As I sat next to the window, I tried to distract my mind from all the pain. The situation and sorrows of all those people hurt me, and it pained me how alone I was at that moment. No hand to wave at me. No face to smile encouragingly.

Twenty minutes later, the final whistle blew, and the train began to chug slowly. Its rusty joints groaned, as if thousands of ropes in the hands of the families tugged them back, trying in vain to stop its forward movement. But the train exhaled an angry moan, shook itself off, then quickly took off down the track.

The train carriages were filled to the brim: soldiers, students, farmers, widows, teenagers, and workers, while vendors wandered through the cars loudly hawking tea, toothbrushes, tissues, and cigarettes. Two seats away from me, young lovers whispered intimately. Perhaps the girl preferred riding the train with her boyfriend so she could capture a few extra moments of closeness before the lances of war carried him off. Or perhaps they were newlyweds who had decided to spend their honeymoon somewhere or another, the way people had done before the war. If only I were in that boyfriend's place. If only a hand were calming me or a heart were crying for my sake, and I could feel its warmth giving me the strength to remain steadfast in the face of all the bullshit that awaited me. But alas! How could an emotionally debilitated creature such as myself experience and taste such love?

The train stopped at the next station. I got off and stood bewildered among the masses. I didn't know where to walk or what to do. I looked around several times, examining all the faces. Surely, I would see a face I knew and could take comfort in it. I kept looking, but in vain. I caught sight of a soldier standing next to a lamppost talking on his phone. I made my way over and waited nearby. When he finished his call, I went closer and quickly said, "Good morning!"

He returned the greeting coolly.

"How do I get to the conscription centre?"

"Why are you looking for that?"

"I'm a new conscript."

I finished talking and showed him my notice. He took a quick glance, folded it, and handed it back to me. Gesturing to the east he said, "The conscription centre is over there in the Istiqbal Camp."

"Is it close?"

"No. No. You have to take a taxi."

He finished talking, then pulled me by the arm for several steps. He pointed toward the parking lot outside the train station which was about three hundred metres away. He said, "From there, take a taxi. Tell the driver to take you to Istiqbal Camp."

I thanked him and headed over. From the parking lot, I took a broken-down Hilux truck driven by a farmer who never stopped griping. He transported me out of town and stopped in front of a small local market filled with farmers, chicken sellers, tea vendors, and falafel shops. The crank of a driver pointed toward a vast cornfield and said: "Istiqbal Camp and the conscription centre are over there. Way back there. About 200 metres past the well dug by the Chinese."

I got out of the car, a cold wind whipping at my face. I cut through the hustle and bustle of the market and walked for several minutes into an open area. I stopped to gaze across at the sprawling fields. A meddlesome question ran through my mind: What kind of conscription centre is located in corn fields and past a well?

Confusion swirled around me. How could it not? I was a rookie who might easily be drowned in an inch of water. Perplexed, I turned and looked around several times, searching for the start of the trail I should take.

However, given the choice between taking a risk or waiting around, I opted to wait beside an old lamppost covered in layers of advertisements and pictures of those killed in war. My wait didn't last long. Soon, other taxis stopped at the market, and a number of people got out. Seeing an opportunity, the sellers tenaciously showed off their wares. The new arrivals ignored it all and traipsed through the dense cornfields without any hesitation or indecision. I ran to catch up with the last person before he slipped among the tall stalks of corn. We walked between and through fields, wading into mud and thorns, and received the nastiest of curses from farmers who grew so angry they started to hurl rocks at us.

At the end of the long walk, we found ourselves in front of a large rusty door covered by layer upon layer of martyrs' photos topped with ripped, sun-faded flags. The gate and everything around it was fortified with cement barriers and sandbag barricades.

There was no sign anywhere to indicate what it was, but we knew from the whispers working their way around that this was the gate of Istiqbal Camp. In times past, it had been the headquarters of a German company, Bananas Firma, that had operated under the cartel in the area. In this valley, they had established one of the biggest plantations in the country but, after abandoning it, the army took over the site and hadn't added one thing to it since. Even now the doors bore signs in German. As for the gigantic warehouses, they were used as soldiers' barracks and depots while the eighteen villas—built with high-quality Swedish wood impervious to termites—housed officers and served as a headquarters for the intelligence division and the higher-ups.

All the annexes were constructed with red stucco that had been eaten away by the passing years and war. They looked out onto a broad square courtyard; its outer border was fenced in by a red brick wall with brambles that covered most of its surface, while the inner edge was walled off by eucalyptus trees. Not much in the way of equipment remained in the camp, except for a rusted-out medical cart overrun by shrubbery. Aside from that, it was just stacks of old barbed wire with thousands of discarded plastic shopping bags caught on it, a pile of torn sheet metal, and some twisted iron bars. At the centre of the field a flagpole had been erected. Dangling from it was a banner, chewed up over months by the sun, wind, and rain, and then spat back out withered, torn, and faded.

I expected that we would be the first to arrive and was surprised to find it already swarming with people who had come from various parts and from all social classes. With nothing else to do for the moment, I wandered about aimlessly, scrutinizing faces.

Amid the forest of faces and bodies, I saw him with his Asiatic features and long, coal-black hair that reached his eyes. Everyone called him the "son of the Vietnamese woman." His mother and her family had fled Saigon in the 1960s before it fell into the hands of the Northern Vietnamese and were at risk of being stranded. American warships had transported them by the thousands and dropped them off on the coastlines of this country.

For years, his mother lived in a Vietnamese refugee camp, until some sense of stability flowed back into their lives and she could leave the camp. Settling in our town, she opened a popular restaurant that served our own local dishes. Nobody had a clue when or where she had learned to prepare them so expertly. Eventually, she got married and gave birth to two boys and many girls, but nobody knew their names due to the family's isolation.

My eyes remained fixed on him. I hadn't seen a single face that I knew or was even acquainted with in this whole place except for his. The "son of the Vietnamese woman" was smoking like a chimney while talking to someone else. I considered walking over, but in the end I decided not to get involved with him, since problems had a way of trailing him everywhere he went. His name had been connected to so many catastrophes. I mention this because we were classmates in middle school, and I recalled that he had a younger brother who used to play violent sports and followed him around like a shadow.

During the first years of the war, he and his brother left our town and took up residence in hotspots throughout the country where they profiteered off the war. What was the exact nature of their business? Selling munitions and transporting them? Gun running? Tracking down those lost, detained, or otherwise kidnapped in confrontation zones? Perhaps they were middlemen?

When skirmishes broke out and pressure increased on one side or the other, circumstances became favourable for business. The weaker side would always pay higher prices to get supplies. Through a rather hazy process, the older brother received orders and gave them to the younger one, who had recently become quite addicted to parkour. He would prepare the order, then pack it in his knapsack. At the height of the confrontations and embargo, he would run, jump, and somersault over the rubble and bombed-out houses and break through the lines of demarcation to deliver the package to his intended goal. Then, carrying the money he had picked up, he would backtrack the same way he had come.

The operation repeated itself several times a day until he had delivered all the orders. This didn't mean that the "son of a Vietnamese woman" was a big boss by any stretch of the imagination. Certainly not. This business transcended him and went beyond the limits of his ability or knowledge and relationships. He and his brother were simply two links in a long chain that stretched from east to west. A chain that respected neither boundaries, nor areas of influence, nor even front lines, but was indispensable to all sides.

During one Eid al-Fitr, hostilities broke out unexpectedly. Pressure intensified on the front and the younger brother had to make a drop. After he received the order from the older brother, he packed his bag, hoisted it on his back, and took off into the fiery skirmish. He ran, crawled, and somersaulted over the rubble and ruined houses. While jumping off the end of a wall of a destroyed building that separated him from his goal, a sniper's bullet pierced his skull, splattering its contents as his body tumbled down and collapsed into a heap in a narrow alleyway. It lay there for months. Nobody dared retrieve his body, which in any case had disappeared after dogs and worms had thoroughly mangled it. After that event, the mother closed her house, shut down her restaurant, and left our town for some unknown destination. I have no idea where this guy turned up from just now.

Recruits wandered the field aimlessly. Most of the offices were locked and the place itself was empty of officers and soldiers, except for one tall soldier whose wrinkled face was pockmarked by chickenpox and decades of poor shaving. He wore a filthy winter military uniform that lacked even a zipper and plastic sandals with woollen socks riddled with holes. He sat on a rock next to the chassis of an ancient Mercedes. Silent and dejected, he smoked and sipped his morning coffee from a metal container while his small eyes stared blankly, betraying his misery, poverty, and a bout of hepatitis.

The relentless weight of time pushed me to sit beside one of the trees as soldiers and officers began to arrive in throngs. Hunger gnawed away at me, so I opened my bag and pulled out a biscuit. I took a bite. The smell of my mother swelled within me, and I heard my father say in a voice filled with tears, "May God make you content, my son."

Cold goosebumps crawled across me. All the tears of the world welled in my eyes, and I pushed down the boulders and weights that had lodged in my throat and brought me to the brink of suffocation. I ignored this feeling and fought against it, but it overcame me, forcing me to cough and spit up what was in my mouth.

Someone sitting near me pulled out a bottle of water from his bag and tossed it toward me. I took a quick gulp and gave it back. Wiping away my tears, I sized him up. I found a heavyset guy with shoulders that carried a large head, which didn't quite fit with the rest of his body. I began to say something to him, but a clamour rose up along the edges of the courtyard and I got up to see what was going on.

Perched high on a chair, one of the soldiers let out a long whistle. Everyone came toward him, looking up, as others craned their necks and waited for what he had to say. He looked across the faces and blew the whistle again, cursing under his breath before welcoming the newcomers in a loud voice. He then began a vapid speech on soldiering, the Nation, and brothers-in-arms. When he finished, he let out a long sigh and uttered another quiet curse. Afterward, he started to explain how registration would proceed: we would begin by taking a personal information form from the window at the reception desk, followed by filling in the required data, and finally receiving a card and temporary number.

When the soldier finished talking, people shoved one another out of the way and crowded in front of the window to take the four-page form. Amid that suffocating melee, you had to look past the profanity, accompanying blows, crushing of feet, and violent clinging together of bodies in order to concentrate on the young soldier's hand dropping the forms in front of us. Everyone who succeeded in retrieving a form had equal difficulty extricating themselves from the masses.

We began filling it out—a matter not without considerable uncertainty and perplexity, during which we had to resort to asking our comrades for help. Some attached their picture to the form with tape, others used a stapler, while others used gum or a paperclip. Nobody cared about the method as much as they cared about affixing their photo so the young soldier would take the form back.

When a conscript finished, he scurried off, shoving himself headlong once again into the pile of writhing bodies. It was a chaotic commotion of thronging, clinging, and swearing. Bodies heaved against one another and none of the officers tried to organize the process. Most were content merely to observe while others closed their office doors for the day and left.

After everyone had submitted their forms, we waited. Finally, one of the soldiers from the office came out carrying a stack of cards. His eyes roved among our faces for a few seconds before he placed the stack on the ground and began distributing the cards. Bodies scrambled over one another while arms became interlocked and interlaced. In the end, I got a card that had nothing more than the number "936" written on it in a thick pen.

At 11:30 am, we were ordered via microphone to fall into line. When we had done so, the tall soldier with the crude mouth and trembling limbs came up and began to count us off, one by one. Conscripts were divided into three groups, each made up of forty individuals. Exhausted and in a deplorable state, we stood in wavy ranks as dizziness struck us and the sun beat down on our necks.

After more waiting, a truck approached from inside the camp and stopped in front of us. Four soldiers climbed on top and began distributing uniforms to the right of the truck and shoes to the left. It was up to each of us to fight and hurl ourselves into the fray, kicking and headbutting and crawling over others, in order to get a uniform and then repeat the process to get shoes. And it didn't end there. The soldiers didn't know our sizes ahead of time and were simply liquidating their storage. Each conscript had to exchange with another for the right fit, which required an arduous search. Those who couldn't make a trade with another person had no choice but to go to the warehouse and look for their size.

After everyone had gotten kitted out with a military uniform and shoes, we were divided into barracks that had previously been employed as ware-

houses for the German company. I found myself and twenty-two other conscripts in Barracks #1, which was nothing more than a long hangar with
brick walls worn away by bullets and time. Its roof was covered with sheet
metal scarred with holes, the centre of which had a large opening equal in
circumference to a crater in the ground of the warehouse itself. Along the
interior walls—which had been last painted some 19 years ago—cracks and
holes were arrayed alongside dark black splotches. In the corners and on
the floor, there were armies of ants and crickets, piles of rat droppings, bird
feathers, and hay. After a while, we realised what the black splotches were.
One of the soldiers who came to show us where the blankets were informed
us that a stray mortar shell had come through the roof of the barracks about
a month ago and detonated as it hit the ground, killing eight people asleep
on cots and splattering their blood and body parts onto the roof and walls.

I went to a corner of the barracks where there was a pile of sheets and
blankets. The stench of mildew mixed with rat excrement wafted through
the air. The filthiness of the bedding its smell shocked me, but there was no
alternative. Everyone jockeyed and competed for the available awfulness. I
lowered my head, thinking for a few moments, then I did what everyone else
had done. I hurled my body into the crowd and began searching among that
mountain of filth. I snatched what I thought was clean and good enough
and got out of the crush of humanity. I heard someone clear their throat and
a familiar voice call out, "You!"

Perplexed, I turned toward the source of the sound. I saw that heavyset
guy who had given me a bottle of water standing a few steps away, smiling.
He came toward me and with that smile still etched on his face and said,
"Good afternoon! I'm Suleiman."

I forced myself to smile. Hesitantly, I returned his greeting and introduced myself. I tried to muster the desire to chat at length, but found myself
backing up slowly. I left him and went to look for a decent bed. The only
cot I could find was underneath the gash in the roof beside the window. Its

frame was broken, but it did the job and provided a decent view of the camp courtyard. I think everyone had avoided choosing that spot out of fear of the hole that continuously reminded and warned us that we too could be next. Or perhaps it was an attempt to escape altogether from the memory and nightmares of those who had died there. I didn't care. I found the cot in that spot acceptable, and it provided me with a sense of privacy that was unavailable elsewhere in the barracks.

Night fell. In one of the corners of the barracks, a lamp shone, covered by a blue shade, and it filled our surroundings with a demoralizing blue light. A captain in the military police entered and ordered us to shave our heads. At first, we didn't know what to do. Eyes glanced across faces, confused and searching for answers. When the captain noticed our baffled expressions, he impatiently shouted: "Everyone will shave his buddy. We want you in line tomorrow morning!"

He turned around and walked out. For a few moments, murmurs arose. Then scissors and blades were brandished, and hair began to fall. Scalps shone. After I got buzzed, I felt my head. For the first time in my life, it had been turned into a cold, smooth cue ball.

I went back to my cot. The place reeked of the stench of bodies and breath, fleas and mosquitoes. I tried to close my eyes but failed. I was filled with the overwhelming sense that my eyelids had disappeared, and my body had become a plank of wood covered by a layer of taut skin. Through the opening in the roof, I continued to stare at the sky and stars. My first night in the grave would not be unlike this one, with all its darkness, desolation, and insomnia. And if not, then I must now be resting at the bottom of the earth, my body and mind ravaged by all the pain of the world.

In this hopeless moment, I didn't know whether I was troubled about what was to come, or worried that a missile could fall on the barracks at any moment. Or maybe I was concerned that a plane would attack the camp and blow everything to smithereens. Or worried about an impending ground attack on the camp. I didn't know. But if a ground attack *did* take place, how would we confront it? We had no weapons and, even if we did, most of us wouldn't have a clue how to use them. I bet we would run into the darkness and wasteland, fleeing confrontation and certain death. Yes, we would run and run. And it would be known that the soldiers deserted their camp and fled into the desert and darkness. Oh God, when will this night end?

I don't know when sleep finally overtook me, but a nightmare crept in, and I screamed out in panic. I woke up immediately and sat bolt upright, staring terrified into the darkness and stars. Deep within the enveloping blackness, a light flickered. I saw Suleiman's face grow bright for a few seconds, illuminated by an orange flame, then the darkness swallowed it up just as quickly. Afterward, I saw the smouldering ember of his cigarette glow red, lighting up his face then dying out once more.

I collected my thoughts and began to get out of bed. Before I could, I heard a strange whistling sound, then a forceful impact. Gravel scattered across the floor and throughout the courtyard. I bolted out of bed. The sound repeated, followed by a flash that lit up the barracks and faces before crashing into the wall. Sparks shot off everywhere, flooding the courtyard with an incandescent red light. A buzz rose up among us. Suddenly, a red blaze pierced the roof, tearing through it from one end to the other and slamming into the opposite wall, where it let out a gigantic boom. Sparks and gravel flew in every direction. Bodies fell over one another and someone yelled out in panic, "They're attacking the camp! Brace yourselves!"

I laid down on the ground and protected my head with my arms. Shouts and whining rose up and, at this moment, my mother's voice resounded in my head, warning: "Be a coward, my son! Be a coward!"

I shoved my body under the bed. Panicked conscripts kept bumping into each other, fleeing, stumbling over one another, and scurrying away.

The corners and hiding places were too narrow and one of them yelled out, "Turn out the lights! Get on the floor!"

One of the soldiers hurled a rock at the lamp and the barracks were drowned in inky darkness. Fiery missiles continued to rain down on the camp, ploughing into the ground and ripping apart roofs. Walls split open and sparks and shrapnel flew off every which way. I was scared. Panicked. I sobbed, quivering like a small child or sparrow. It was as if I were in a dream or watching a movie, or as if someone were telling me an unbelievable story.

One of the conscripts grew hysterical. He ran out of his hiding place and into the courtyard. We heard him screaming into the oncoming bullets and at the sky and walls. He called out to everyone who had previously done him wrong and cursed them with the vilest of curses. I left my hiding place and carefully peered out the window. I saw him in only his underwear, walking confusedly around the field, gesturing belligerently with his arms. He cursed an "Abu Rami" through the barrage of bullets whizzing by on his right and left. Sparks flew around him and a red cloud lit up his face. Shouts for him to come inside or to lay prostrate on the ground rose up, but he paid them no attention. He left everything behind and ran toward the bullets, seeking revenge against Abu Rami. When his voice fell silent, I went back to my hiding spot, shaken and terrified. I asked the darkness: Was he killed? How did it happen? Did this wretched guy suffer? And where is his corpse now?

The scene seemed to last an unbearably long time, as if it were a month, a year, or maybe even a century. Each second was pain and terror. In reality, though, it was no longer than half an hour. Immediately after, everything quieted down. Several minutes later, the hum of incoherent talking and questions rose. We carefully left our hiding places and all met in the courtyard.

Shock and fear were visible on our faces. One was sobbing while another swore, and still others vowed to desert. Many couldn't even stand or walk, they were so affected by the shock and terror of it all. Bullets had ripped apart the roofs and walls but hadn't killed anyone. This was just the beginning of more to come. Our first rendezvous with war. The officers warned us against gathering in groups, but no one heeded it. We heard a soldier say, pointing to a far-off plateau west of the encampment, "It came from over there. That's why we didn't hear them fire."

Another soldier came forward, carrying the remnants of a rocket he had extracted from one of the walls. He waved it in our faces and said, "24 calibre. They attacked us with these."

None of us uttered a word. We just calmed ourselves by silently damning them deep in our hearts. Suddenly, the conscript who had run out to face the bullets came out of nowhere. He stood in front of us, panting, then angrily said, "Abu Rami. It's Abu Rami. He lends money to the needy then takes their girls."

The conscripts circled him and, as his insanity reached its peak, the group broke up, leaving him alone in the field, wandering in circles and asking, "So you don't believe me, eh? You don't believe me?!"

Help never came. It was as if what we had just experienced concerned no one in the world but us.

Not even a single ambulance arrived.

We remained in the courtyard for hours, then headed back to the barracks, filling it with our muttering. Suddenly and without warning, a thunderclap echoed, and the sky opened up. The rain was torrential, and water flooded the ground, causing insects, lice, and rats to flee their holes.

Dressed only in what we had, we gathered around, trying to warm ourselves with our breath and body heat as we attempted to light a fire but failed. Water poured in and soaked everything we tried to ignite. We kept waiting. And, as we did, the cold and wet joined our growing sense of desperation and helplessness, crushing us. All we could do was hope the rain would stop.

Chapter 6

Naji Awad

January 3

The first day

Naji Awad awoke with difficulty to the whipping of the wind against the open window. His eyes scanned the dishevelled room. His wife, Fathiya, wasn't beside him as he sat on the edge of his bed. The acidity of last night's wine caused him to belch. He looked at his wristwatch sitting on the nightstand and panicked that it was past 1:15 in the afternoon. He shouted angrily:

– Fucking bitch.

He shaved his beard, got cleaned up, and then proceeded to make himself a cup of coffee. He added a bit of cold milk and sat in the living room, smoking and sipping. He stared at an erotic poster on the opposite wall, which was based on one of the stories in *One Thousand and One Nights*. Suddenly, the face he had noticed at the Al-Niqash residence flickered within him. He felt that the situation was taking a new direction—a direction he did not know or had been unfamiliar with before.

He drank two more cups of coffee and took some aspirin before putting on his clothes. After a spritz of cologne, he got ready to head out. Before he could open the door, he felt his side and discovered that he had forgotten his revolver. He returned to his bedroom and searched for it between the nightstand and pillow. When he found it, he slid it into his waistband and left.

A quarter of an hour later, he was standing at the front gate of the Al-Niqash residence. Glancing around the courtyard, he pushed the rusty gate open. He saw Muhi Al-Deen Al-Niqash sitting on his chair beneath the grapevine, whittling away on a piece of wood. He walked toward him and said:

– Good morning!

Al-Niqash didn't pay him the least bit of attention. He repeated his greeting, but Al-Niqash looked like someone who neither heard nor saw. He only raised his piece of wood and blew sawdust in his face. He recoiled and began to dust off what had latched onto his clothing. Just then, the door of the Al-Niqash home opened. He saw a woman, crowned by blackness, making her way out. He moved forward and stood in front of her, a frown on his face. From behind her veil, she confidently asked:

– How can we help you, good Sir?

He pointed at her with a finger of someone not used to respecting anyone who stood in front of him:

– Are you Umm Ziad Al-Niqash?

She nodded in the affirmative and said:

– Yes.

He extended a hand to shake hers. However, his hand remained suspended in the void for several moments before pulling back and sliding into his pants pocket. Umm Ziad would not give him any chance to put her in an awkward position or to loiter longer than necessary. She said:

– How can we help you, Mr. Officer?

Only in that instant did he realise he didn't know what he wanted. And, even if he did, he didn't know how to begin speaking. He thought about reversing course and coming back later, but that would be embarrassing. Standing there, he grumbled then said the first thing that came to his mind:

– Did your son travel today?

–Yes.

Her blunt response closed off all the doors to dialogue that he had intended to open. But could that render a man such as himself incapable of achieving his objective? He was used to concocting stories. Over the previous four decades, he had become hooked on taking advantage of opportunities as they presented themselves. Al-Niqash, who at that moment was sanding a piece of lemon wood, took a quick glance at him. Naji said softly:

– You could have postponed his trip or even exempted him from going altogether!

Just then, Al-Niqash stopped sanding the wood and remained glued to his seat, not lifting his eyes from his hands. Umm Ziad called out, concerned:

– How?!

Naji Awad pushed his hands into his pants pockets and, before he could respond, she added with a clear plea:

–Show us how! He is our one and only, and the provider for our family. And, as you can see, his father is ill!

When he heard her words, he gave a triumphant smile from deep within his soul. His manoeuvring had hit its intended target. Some of the barriers and walls of this family had begun to crumble, and he had a pretext for sticking his foot inside their home. He affected a smile and said:

– I'm here for that very reason!

He spread his hand out toward the old man sitting on his chair and added:

– I will help you get your boy back as soon as possible!

Umm Ziad thanked him, and he passed her a card with his number, and she gave him the full name of her son. Then, after inspecting the door, windows, and openings in the blinds with greedy eyes, he headed out.

When he got to the police station, he was surprised by the number of cars. He made his way into the station just as one of the policemen informed him that an inspection committee was visiting. His whole body shook. Not everything in the precinct was on the up and up, and he was unable to make his way to the police chief's office.

He remained waiting in the lobby, smoking and collecting his thoughts until he had regained his cool, although neither was the reason behind his calm. He simply remembered that the station chief would bear all responsibility, and he would be the one to be questioned or blamed.

He knocked on the door and made his way into the office, pushing himself through a cloud of smoke and body odour. He waited around for about fifteen minutes before he realised that the security apparatuses were trying to monitor the disbursement of humanitarian aid to those entitled to it—something that touched upon his interests to a certain degree. He wasted no time and stepped out of the meeting unnoticed. He then made a number of calls to people inside and outside the town.

That evening, he sat alone at his night-time haunt, smoking and drinking black tea, as he filled his gullet with plates of beans and hot peppers. Antar walked in and informed him that someone was waiting for him outside. He got up from the table and returned moments later carrying a stuffed envelope. His night companions started to gather around and, as the place began to fill up, so did the table. The night's activities could commence.

It wasn't his lucky day or night, and he lost most of his cash. He pulled out the last two bills from the envelope and shoved them into his pocket. Then he tossed the empty envelope between his feet and got up from the table to go smoke in a corner near the window by himself. Bathed in the light of an unknown source, which was coming from the barren hillside, he looked out at the tombstones.

His phone rang. He stared vacantly at the unidentified number. He thought about ignoring it as he normally did with unknown numbers, but in an instant he made up his mind and answered. A voice came through:

– Good evening, Sir!

The voice roused him from his distraction and brought him back to reality. He returned the greeting and the woman quickly said:

– I wanted to remind you of the matter of Ziad, like you asked.

– Ah. Okay. You did. I will see what I can do.

– We will await a call from you. And don't worry. Your troubles will be compensated. We just want our son to return!

– I will do my utmost. Wait for a call from me!

He hung up and put the phone back in his pocket. The matter at hand had started to head in an unplanned direction.

Antar approached and asked:

– So, how are you going to return the Al-Niqash boy from the frontlines?

He turned to him and blew out smoke from his cigarette, then said:

– We'll see. We'll figure something out.

Antar lit his cigarette:

– The war devours people and stones. No soldier can be returned from the front. It's not like it was before.

Naji interrupted, waving a hand:

– Shhhh. Enough, enough! I know that.

– But you said...

– I said, I only said... I will say what I want. Who's going to hold me to what I say?

Antar let out a guffaw:

– Ah, I got it.

Silence filled the air for a few moments. Antar forced out a cough and then, rolling his cigarette between his fingers, he said:

– The shortest path to a goal is a straight line. Why don't you just be direct with them and save yourself all this effort and thought, unless of course this matter isn't as frivolous as you say.

He turned toward him and went on staring for a few seconds then pointed to him:

– You're right.

Truth be told, it wasn't that Naji Awad was falling in love with the Al-Niqash daughter, as all circumstances might indicate. Rather, he wanted a child. A child to carry his name and guarantee that his dynasty would continue. That was all there was to it. Yet his mind hadn't absorbed that desire, or, more precisely, he couldn't deal with it or express it as such.

How could he? As it was, he was faced with overlapping problems that were impossible to solve one by one. First of all, he was impotent. Second, there was his interminable connection to his wife Fathiya, and third, his past and his present. Even if all these problems were solved, would the Al-Niqash family accept that their daughter live in a sexless marriage? That her womb would become a vessel into which doctors planted his sperm in order to harvest a child? And would his wife, Fathiya, be alright with that, after she had lost hope of being a mother and a woman?

So many questions filled his mind, it was like a balloon about to pop. He left everything behind and walked out earlier than normal. He didn't like to use cars to get around except under duress. Walking through the dimly lit streets, he stopped to relieve his bladder against the trunk of a tree. After he finished, he heard the shouting of an irate woman that sounded a great deal like the screams of his wife. He didn't heed it and kept walking along the empty pathways. He stopped for a few moments in front of the Al-Niqash residence. He lit a cigarette and calmly puffed away while peering intently at the house, which was submerged in darkness. At that instant, he made a decision that he intended to execute in the morning.

He arrived home and found his wife in the entryway, standing among a pile of cosmetics and beauty products. She was smoking and wearing a negligee, as she usually did. She shot him a look, then moved toward one of the corners and began to empty out a large bag filled with cartons. He closed the door and tossed his keys on a nearby side table. He got out of his clothes at the bathroom door, turned on the water for the tub, and stood in front of a wide mirror. He poured bath salts into the water along with some fragrant herbs, and then went back to open a small fridge and take out a few small flasks of an alcoholic beverage, which he emptied into a big metal cup. He placed some ice cubes in it, took a gulp, and brought it with him to the bathtub.

As he lay in it, the water slowly filled up. Steam and the scent of fragrant herbs billowed up, and he closed his eyes. It seemed as if he were listening to a far-off call. A strong urge to smoke overcame him, but a kind of paralysis had seeped into his body. His limbs felt heavy and rigid. His wife opened the bathroom door and was surprised by the scene. He opened his eyes. He saw her standing there in front of the door, the light of the entryway revealing the intimate parts of her body. She ignored him and moved toward the cabinet. Then, in one movement, she took off her henna-stained clothes and set them aside. She wet a cleaning rag and began to wipe away the traces of the brown ink from her neck and chest before putting on different clothes and leaving without a single word.

His mind replayed the scene, re-imagining the sight of the large surgical scar in the shape of an upside down cross in the middle of her abdomen. He regained his strength and fought back the dizziness. Getting up from the bath, he made his way toward the cabinet and pulled out a packet of cigarettes. He lit one and went back into the tub, where he took another swig of his drink. The numbness returned to his senses and, in that moment, his mind fixated on his wife and on that horrendous surgical scar. He heard her voice greeting someone outside. He closed his eyes and tried to recall an erotic memory of that body. He succeeded—but it wasn't a clear memory. Just faded devoid of both colour and emotion.

***

Of all the previous and subsequent events of his life, he remembered–

with unusual clarity–a Saturday in December some thirteen years ago. The memory of that Saturday always crept out of nowhere during moments of quiet, when his mind would drift back to it. He remembered all the details, even those others might think had no value. Such as the blue ink stain below his shirt pocket and the tightness of his belt, or the acidity of his stomach, the new 50-franc note in his pocket, and the face of the soldier who opened the prison gate to let him drive out in his Volga. He also remembered the striking of the town clock, announcing the 2 o'clock hour.

At that time, Fayrouz sang on the radio airwaves and the roads were jammed. He made a detour down a side road in his car that didn't have a license number, except for a black plate with the letter "P" written in a thick white script, nothing else. The side street was empty and unusually devoid of life. He didn't really notice and found it an opportunity to take his car for a real spin. Suddenly, the left-front tyre exploded, and the vehicle spun around. In vain, he tried to control it. Within microseconds, he saw the face of an older homeless man who stood on the sidewalk beside a barrel fire. He could see the man's eyes and a grin filled with schadenfreude work its way across his rotting teeth. The car violently crashed into the wall of a driving school. His head hit the steering wheel, and his backbone cracked loudly. He tasted blood in his mouth and raised his head from the steering wheel. As he wiped away the blood from his face, he saw what appeared to be apparitions running toward him. The figures transformed into people wielding clubs. He stared at them in shock. One guy tried to pry open the car door but couldn't. With his club, he broke through what was left of the windshield glass. He then grabbed Naji's shirttail and yanked him outside. When he fell onto the ground, the clubs and kicking descended upon him. Faces blurred and he heard names he would never forget his entire life. He didn't know how he withstood all that or when he finally lost consciousness. He also didn't know why those people assaulted him or why they had left him alive. Involuntarily and unconsciously, this incident forever made him hate driving cars or even riding in them.

He finally opened his eyes after ten days on a bed in the police hospital. He found himself with a broken neck, a punctured skull, and two broken arms. These were the visible injuries, and there were others that nobody noticed, like an internal injury to his right buttock that developed into a deep abscess after several months, as well as a crack in his lower femur. That was the last injury he recovered from. After forty-five days, his wife visited him in his hospital bed. The recovery period had managed to resolve most of his pains. They talked at length before she closed the door and tried to seduce him with caresses. He felt a fire ignite inside him. He kissed and fondled her, but his member did not respond and just stayed limp like a silicone thumb. After a number of attempts, they surrendered to failure and attributed it to the precarious state of his health and the side effects of some of the medication. They repeated the attempt several weeks later, but with the same result. He complained about the problem to one of his doctors, who ran some tests—only for the doctor to inform him that he had lost his ability forever.

After he was discharged from the hospital, he remained a prisoner in his house for months on end. When a letter from the Surveillance and Investigation Unit of the Ministry of Interior required it, he returned to his work in the prison. But the man who returned was not the same one who had departed months before. He had become wild and ferocious. Deep suspicion toward everyone engulfed him, and naturally his wife received the brunt of it and his cruelty.

Two years after the accident, while in a state of intoxication, he returned to his house one day to find his wife waiting for him. He was surprised to see her dressed to the nines. She was talking on the phone and waved at him before turning her back. In fact, she had been waiting for him to celebrate their wedding anniversary and had made special preparations. Like usual, he had completely forgotten the occasion and had an altogether different perspective.

He made his way to the kitchen and opened the fridge. He took out a bottle of beer, cracked it open, and drank while listening to her talk on the phone. She was speaking to the woman teaching her cosmetology. She had told him months ago that she wanted to learn this trade, but how could he know if she was really talking to a woman or if it was nothing more than a ruse to disguise how she'd been caught off guard by him coming home early? His mind was bedevilled.

After she ended her call, he set the bottle in the refrigerator and walked toward her, grabbed her wrist, and dragged her forcefully toward the bedroom. He found the bedroom decorated with red lights, perfume, and candles. He looked past it all and threw her onto the bed. She smiled, imagining she was one of his sex toys. When she sat up to say something seductive, he smacked her suddenly and handcuffed her to the bedframe. Opening the dresser, he pulled out two neckties and tied her feet to the bed. She gave a thrilled laugh. He left her and went into the bathroom to get a razor blade and came back. By now, she was gyrating on the bed and her smile didn't vanish until he taped her mouth shut. At that moment, she saw evil dance across his eyes. She tried to cry out but couldn't. He didn't waste any time. He mounted her, pinning her down with the weight of his body, and buried his rough fingers into her vulva and cut off her clitoris.

No, he didn't deny that he loved her. And perhaps her love was the only stable thing in his tumultuous life. However, he feared he would lose her. She likewise loved him despite it all. He was all that was left for her in this world. She was unbothered by his impotence and had decided to stay with him and adapt to it. True, some days were difficult for them both, but despite the difficulty, it didn't snuff out the love inside of her or her feeling of duty toward him. He on the other hand wanted to free her of any pressure that could influence her to stay with him but also wanted to block her only way out.

One day, Fathiya was crying like never before in her whole life. True, she was physically in pain but her mental anguish was weightier and more serious. She considered what happened to her from a different angle, fixated primarily on his malice and the lack of trust. However, despite it all, she accepted the matter and was satisfied to live a celibate life with him. What mattered to her up until that moment was that she was with him and that was enough.

When she heard that the local hospital was conducting in vitro fertilization, she grabbed his hand, and they went to the hospital to run tests. A lovely female doctor informed them that there was a high probability that the operation would be a success, but she asked for a large sum of money that went way beyond all their savings. They had no other choice but to work hard to save up. He hustled and did everything that was legal and not so legal while she worked diligently to dispense with numerous items from their grocery and shopping lists. As days passed, their savings began to approach what they needed for the operation, but things didn't progress as they had wanted. A year and three months after mutilating her clitoris, she experienced a strange pain in her side, which finally led to removal of her uterus entirely in a hospital that was owned by an Indian doctor working illegally in the country. The operation deprived her of all hope of living as a woman, and she imprisoned herself in her room for weeks, grave-faced and lost in thought, not saying a single word.

When she had recovered from the silence and isolation, she left her room but had become an altogether different woman. Nothing remained of her former personality. The change she experienced was violent and stormy in a way that no one had expected. Constantly agitated, she screamed all the time. Curse words streamed from her mouth relentlessly. She behaved as if the Indian doctor had removed her fear and uterus together. She didn't hesitate to clash with Naji Awad and the situation reached a point where she would brandish a weapon in his face. She did this numerous times, but despite all that, she couldn't leave him. Or, to be more precise, he had brought her to the point of no return that he had wanted all along. His fate was tied to hers forever.

During this time, he paid bribes to the Ministry of Interior to transfer him to the police station in his hometown and used the money they had saved for the operation to renovate and expand the old shoemaker's house. As days went by, the normalcy of marital life between them dissolved into nothing, and their silent and mundane life began, devoid of even the slightest trace of feeling.

This isn't to say she had moved on from everything in the past. Not at all. He had seen her crying on more than one occasion without an apparent reason, and she often blamed him for what he had done. She would threaten him, but he didn't pay it much attention. As long as he loved her and she loved him, he knew that she would never act on her threats.

***

He lost his train of thought when he heard the door open. Standing there, he saw her in front of the door, the light of the entryway exposing the wrinkles of her body under her silk robe. She was looking him straight in the eye with sheer hate like never before. She took a few slow steps toward him, her hand behind her back. He tried to lift his hand, but it was no use. She came closer. He saw her surgical scar and her fist tightly gripping the handle of a large knife. He tried to move but was completely paralyzed in the bathtub. She grabbed one of the flasks and threw it into the tub water and smiled. He realised she had poisoned his drink. She removed her covering and he saw the gash where her clitoris had been cut out. He realised she had evil designs and tried to scream or move but couldn't. Saliva spewed from his mouth. She came closer and pressed her hand down on his forehead, drowning him. He gurgled, choking on water. From under the water, he saw the glint of a blade rise, then fall on him.

His whole body shook, and he gasped. He sat up suddenly in the tub and looked around the room with panicked eyes. He didn't find anyone and exhaled and relaxed. He then wiped his face and got out of the tub. At that moment, he heard her voice a ways off, cursing and swearing. He wrapped his body in a generous-sized towel and went into the bedroom.

Just then, his phone rang. Sitting on the side of the bed, he answered. It was one of the officers down at the precinct, informing him that three people had been arrested for possessing a quantity of bootleg alcohol. He asked about its size. When the officer told him that it was no more than eight bottles, he let out a long sigh. He ordered their release and ended the call before throwing the phone off to the side.

He had a little time. He got up and took the computer out of his closet, sat on the bed, and opened YouTube. He flipped through a few songs, but nothing caught his attention and instead began to flip through a porn site. Unexpectedly, he found himself watching a sadistic sex scene. He kept watching closely. Suddenly, he heard the ring of his phone from below the pillow next to him. He shoved his hand under it and pulled out an unfamiliar phone. It wasn't his wife's usual device. On the screen was the name of the caller: Nadia Jaber. He put back the phone and returned to the sadistic scene. The phone rang again and again. A feeling he had known before awoke within him. When the phone fell silent, he grabbed it and connected it to the computer. With the stroke of a key, he downloaded all its contents. Then he returned it to its place. As he began to thumb through the copied files, his own phone rang. He took it and put it to his ear without answering. A gruff voice said:

– Open WhatsApp!

He immediately ended the call and opened WhatsApp. He had received eighteen messages from an overseas number. When he opened them, photos of wooden crates containing war materiel, munitions, and communications equipment stared back at him. He let out a long exhale and wrote: "Await my call!"

He turned off his phone and quickly got dressed, lighting a cigarette as he headed out. He drove his Volga eighteen kilometres outside town and arrived at a village known for its cane located on the outskirts of a brackish swamp. There, several armed men met him, and he walked with them to a thatched hut made of cane and swamp mud.

In fact, this wasn't the first time Naji Awad had gotten caught up in arms trafficking, but it was the first time that he had participated in an operation of this size. He wasn't a dealer in the literal sense of the word, more a middleman between corrupt army officers and the Movement of Revolutionary Liberation. The officers would steal war materiel, and he would supply the customer, taking his cut in the end. For an operation of such a large size, his commission was a number that contained seven zeroes and would make him obscenely wealthy. For this reason, he put all his weight into it. In that darkened hut, he displayed his goods to the buyers, and they agreed on a price. He then made a quick call. The meeting only broke up once all the details had been sorted out.

Chapter 7

The Family of Muhi Al-Deen Al-Niqash

January 3

The first day

That afternoon, my mother was in her usual spot, talking to my uncle Ragheb on the phone. She hadn't touched her coffee, which had become cold and, according to her, dreadful-tasting. Depressed and puffy-eyed, she hadn't stopped daubing her eyes or nose. Then, in the middle of her conversation, she glanced without thought through the window and saw a man standing in front of my father. She was startled. Because her eyesight was slightly weak, she took the phone and made her way over to the window. From there she could see that officer from the Political Guidance Committee, Naji Awad, standing in front of my father under the shade of the grapevine. At that very moment, he was shaking something off his clothing. My uncle Ragheb hadn't stopped talking. Surprised, she cut him off:

– Strange! What does that guy want now?

My uncle Ragheb stayed silent for a few moments, then asked what she meant. She said:

– The officer from Political Guidance is in the inner courtyard. I don't know what he wants. Oh God, let it be something positive.

Her surprise passed to him, and he said:

– What does he want with you all? I'm going to stay on the line so you can tell me what he says.

She said firmly:

– No, no. I'll call you back.

She ended the call, then hitched the tail of her headwrap around her face and muttered something indistinct. Like everyone in town, she knew who officer Naji Awad was, and she knew that the only thing he dragged behind him was calamity. However, she was fearful that his visit had something to do with me, and her fear caused a strong trembling inside her and irregular palpitations of her heart.

She crossed the courtyard toward the officer. She met him and listened to what there was to hear before she went back to her spot and directed her frozen stare at the ground. My older sister Henna placed a cup of coffee in front of her. She raised her eyes and stared for several seconds, unnerving Henna. She then took the phone and dialled my uncle back. His drowsy voice returned to the line. She began to tell him what had happened, and Ragheb informed her that it was impossible to bring any conscript back from the frontlines under any circumstance. He acknowledged that he had resorted to asking his acquaintances in the Ministry of the Interior and Ministry of Defence to get them to take my name off the list but had no luck.

With an earnestness equal to the depth of her sadness, she asked him:

– Even with money?

He fell silent for a few moments. Everyone in the house heard his hesitation. He replied:

– I don't know. But you have to be very careful. Maybe this whole thing is just a con.

– Relax. He won't get anything until Ziad returns.

– Then you don't know what kind of person Naji Awad is.

– I know. I do know. There's no harm in going along with him. I believe what you say, but I have a feeling that the issue isn't Ziad at all, even if the officer tries to make it seem that way.

– So then what is it?

– We'll go along with him for a little while, and we'll see what's behind the mask.

– Be careful. If necessary, I'll call my contacts in the Interior.

– No, no. It's not going to be necessary. I'm confident.

Chapter 8

Naji Awad

January 4

The second day

Around noon.

Naji Awad was sitting in the mayor's home sipping tea, his exhausted eyes staring intently at the rug that hung on the wall and the carpet that sat on the floor. The wrinkled face in front of him began to say:

– Are you serious?

Naji Awad didn't know if he was or not, but he replied:

– Yes, I'm serious.

– Do you think that the Al-Niqash family will agree?

He lit a cigarette, took a glass of tea, and began to tap it involuntarily with his index finger. He thought about the hand that had washed and poured tea into it and placed it on the tray. These visions and imaginings no longer filled him with sadness as they had before. The mayor's voice drew him out of his distraction, and he repeated his question. He raised his eyes and puffed out a cloud of smoke, causing the mayor to cough. Naji Awad said in a knowing tone:

– Old man Al-Niqash is ill. He doesn't even realise what's going on around him. It's been said that everything is in his wife's hands. In any case, dealing with women is easier than dealing with men. Why do you doubt they will agree?

The mayor shook his head and muttered a few words. He then got up and opened the window and stared outside for a few moments. He drew in a deep breath of air and said:

– So what are you asking me to do?

Naji Awad got up and stood beside him. He flicked the butt of his cigarette out the window and shoved his hands into his pockets. He watched a disabled person cross the street in a wheelchair. As the wheels let out a sharp screech, he said:

– What I'm asking is that you go to the Al-Niqash home and speak to them about it. That's all.

The mayor was stunned and felt his throat close. He opened his mouth to gulp whatever air he could. His heart raced. He grasped his chest and cried out in disbelief:

– What?!

Naji Awad pursed his lips and said:

– Just as you heard. Nobody's more suited than you to take on this mission.

The mayor raised his hand in protest:

– But…!

Naji Awad grabbed and lowered the mayor's hand, then smiled half-heartedly. While twisting his index finger against the mayor's chest, he said:

– As I said. No one else can do this mission. I'll wait for your call.

He pulled out a cigarette and lit it, blowing smoke toward the mayor. Continuing in the same vein, he said´

– I'm leaving. Get out of my way!

The town mayor beat him to the door, but with a wave of his hand Naji Awad departed, leaving the mayor to stumble around in confusion.

He paused in front of the mayor's house, put on his sunglasses, and continued on his way. Suddenly, he stopped in front of a woman in her forties who used to work in one of the international banks that had evacuated because of the war. He spoke to her for a few minutes. Pleading and pain were evident on her face, which had suffered at the hand of misfortune and decades of makeup. She opened her purse and pulled out a stack of papers. He turned it over quickly before returning it to her. When the middle-aged lady began to weep, he let out a sigh. He then wrote something on a slip of paper and handed it to her. Before he left, his phone rang, and he answered it and told the caller that he would be there in minutes.

At the police station, he made his way to his office and found a rotund man with a large birthmark on his nose waiting for him. The overweight man got up and greeted Naji Awad with both hands. This man wasn't the one who had recently come to town under the pretext of working as a real estate agent. In fact, he was none other than a pimp of down-on-their-luck, emaciated prostitutes whose bodies had been crushed by poverty and hunger, women he had picked up in various cities. And Naji Awad was not simply a faithful customer. He also provided the pimp with an umbrella of protection to act without consequences or worry. Consequently, he received the warmest of welcomes and hospitality from him. As for the whores, despite his repeated visits, they called him "Mr. Oral," which was a nod to his preference. Or, to be perfectly honest, the upper limit of his sexual ability.

Naji Awad sat behind his desk, a forced smile plastered across his face. There was no need for greetings or kind words between two people connected by such a close relationship. The pimp opened a small bag that sat between his feet. He pulled out three medium-sized cardboard boxes and set them in front of Naji Awad. The officer turned them over in his hands and then placed them off to the side, feigning disinterest. When he asked about their contents, the pimp laughed and informed him that they were American devices that had recently arrived. The pimp took one and loudly translated what was written on the packaging. Up until that moment, Naji Awad had not known what was in the boxes. When he asked the pimp impatiently about the contents, he candidly responded:

– Devices to help those who suffer from impotence.

Naji Awad's pupils dilated, and his face clouded over. Exasperated, he said:

– Who are these devices for?!

Confused, the pimp replied:

– For...for you!

– And who told you that I needed it?

Under normal conditions, his explosive words would have broken the resolve of even the most hardened criminals. But they had no power over this pimp, who had grown used to bargaining with excessive self-confidence, and to highlighting the selling points of his products.

The pimp smiled, and then began to explain to him in a carefree manner that he was only trying to help him savour the true taste of life. He confirmed that the devices were not used only by the infirm. However, if it could help *them*, then it could also double the strength of a healthy man, not to mention the fact that illness was not a defect. As they say, "for every sickness there is a remedy." It would be criminal for a sick person to deny himself the pleasures of life when a treatment was readily available. About a half hour later, the pimp left, having convinced Naji Awad to buy two boxes after explaining at length how to use them.

Naji Awad placed the two devices in his desk drawer. When night began to fall, he headed out to his evening revels. He was first to arrive, but didn't wait long before the others poured in. He played and drank until he was quenched. Then a savage desire awoke within him. He ensconced himself in a corner, smoking and drinking, while watching faces and cards. Sexual fantasies overcame him, and he tilted his head back and closed his eyes as he tried to plunge deeper into them and forget the world.

Suddenly, his phone rang. He lifted it without opening his eyes and listened for a few seconds. Then he opened his eyes. They had transformed into two burning coals, and his face clouded over as if it were the face of the devil. He erupted and upended everything on the table and left the place in a flash.

Chapter 9

The Family of Muhi Al-Deen Al-Niqash

January 4

The second day

In a rare occurrence, a knock came to our door after sunset, puzzling everyone inside the house. While out of the ordinary, this could also happen under normal circumstances, yet the visit of the Political Guidance Officer to our home the day before had awakened a latent alertness in the heart of my mother, who began to scrutinize every possibility. It was inevitable—particularly when Naji Awad and his ilk were dealing with you.

My mother gestured to my sisters to go to their rooms. She went to hers, too, and opened the closet and retrieved an old box draped in blue velvet from the bottom. Emptying its contents on the floor, she removed a piece of fabric that had been folded with care. She set it aside, then put everything back in its place. When she unfolded the wrapping, it revealed an old German pistol that had been her grandfather's. She quickly loaded it with bullets and slipped it into her shirt pocket before she went toward the door. She demanded the knocker identify himself. The mayor's voice, irritated as ever, indicated it was him at the door. Her surprise increased. She had been expecting someone else. She opened the door, her finger on the trigger. The weary face of the mayor looked back at her. He asked to speak with both my mother and father. My mother left him waiting a few moments then allowed him to enter.

In reality, the mayor was not at all convinced of the mission Naji Awad had set him on, but he wasn't in a position to refuse or bow out, so he acquiesced, albeit begrudgingly. Despite all that, he knew full well that the Al-Niqash family would never accept Naji Awad as a son-in-law or his wife, Fathiya, as a first wife. It wasn't just the Al-Niqash family's position, but the entire town's. No exception.

When he had spoken to them about the matter at hand, my father's body trembled, and his face clouded over. As for my mother, she fell silent for a few moments. The mayor thought that she was mulling the idea over, but she didn't hesitate a moment, shaking her head and saying:

– I now understand the meaning of Naji Awad's visit to us yesterday.

Stunned, the mayor shouted:

– He visited you?! I had no idea!

– He visited us and offered to return our son, Ziad, from the front lines. It seems that he wants to tie the issue of Ziad to that of Hinaa!

The mayor waved his hand in front of his face, confused.

– I had no idea. I swear to God.

My mother leaned back, then said:

– Mayor, what begins with lies ends with them, too. In any case, and setting aside the issue of Ziad's return, we do not have any girls to marry off.

The mayor said in a hoarse voice:

– But...!

My mother got up and fixed her gaze on the door before she said decisively:

– You've finished your coffee. Now go!

The mayor's eyes widened, and his body dripped sweat. He set aside his still-full cup of coffee and left, perplexed and stuttering incoherently. At that moment, he cursed himself and cursed Naji Awad, and Al-Niqash and his wife, and the very day he had become the town's mayor.

She slammed the door behind him and went nervously back to her seat. My three sisters crowded into the living room, their faces full of fear. My mother asked them to sit down and she began to drink her coffee without saying a single word. When she had finished, she regained her strength and pieced together what she could of her words and thoughts, then informed everyone that the matter had been put to rest. Nothing would break the bonds of their family.

She didn't really believe that the issue was over and done with, but she couldn't do anything other than say a few words to set the minds of the family at ease. She then surprised everyone by saying:

– Let's see what Ziad is doing now.

She took out her phone and made a call. A recorded voice on the other end informed her that the phone was switched off. She tried twice more, then a third time but had no luck. She set the phone on the small table in front of her. Then, while trying to hide her disappointment, which was bubbling to the surface, she said:

– It seems there isn't coverage where he is.

The mayor returned home. Humiliation crushed him, and he felt violent palpitations in his chest. He pulled out a package of medicine from his pocket and placed a small tablet under his tongue. He then sat in the entryway beneath an old Belgian chandelier that didn't really match the house's decor or furniture. After he had settled down and stillness suffused his body, he grabbed the telephone and called Naji Awad, who at that moment was sitting at his evening gathering.

9 o'clock at night...

Our home was flooded in darkness, and everyone had gone off to sleep—everyone except for my mother. Anxiety weighed heavily on her, preventing her from sleeping and leaving her to stare senselessly at the ceiling. Her fingers continuously clicked the prayer beads. In an instant, she shoved her hand beneath the pillow and felt the revolver. Then she closed her eyes.

She heard the sound of a motorcycle circling the house. It stopped as suddenly as it had begun. Fear immediately washed over her. Before she could react, she heard the sound of a weapon being loaded. Then, without any warning, intense gunfire echoed all around. A blazing fire shattered the windowpane, slamming into the opposite wall. The air filled with the smell of gunpowder and dirt. Terrified, my father bolted up from his bed. Glancing around the room, he began to yell hysterically, just as he had when the first rockets fell on our town.

At first, my mother didn't grasp what was going on, and she screamed out in terror. When she heard the cracking and clattering of glass and furniture in the sitting room, she ran toward the girls' room, dodging flashes of bullets. They were cowering in one of the corners, shouting in panic. She wasted no time and threw her body over them. At that very moment, a volley of bullets crashed through the windowpane and destroyed some of the ceramic dishes that had been placed on a wooden shelf, and they also ripped through the clothes closet.

Bodies convulsed in fear. My mother pulled them closer to her, and then noticed that my father was screaming. Before she could decide on a course of action, everything went still and the motorcycle took off.

Moments of silence were followed by violent knocks at the front door. My mother left the girls and covered her head. She was still shaking. She brought her revolver with her and some ammo, and she took a quick sip of water. As she made her way toward the door, she brandished her gun, expecting an intruder to break in at any moment.

Instead, she heard the voice of one of the neighbours. When she opened the door, she saw him, with his three sons standing behind him, along with a few other neighbours. Some women came over to the house and turned on the lights and sat my mother down on the couch to calm her. The crowd in front of the house grew. My mother regained her composure, then quickly realised bullets had punctured the water tank. Neighbours began to repair the holes with waterproof plugs and placed wooden planks over the broken window.

By the time my mother had thanked them and closed the door behind the last one to leave, it was exactly midnight. She carried my father to the girls' room and everyone slept there on the floor...or at least pretended to.

Chapter 10

Ziad Al-Niqash

January 4

The second day

At 7 o'clock in the morning, the rain finally stopped and the sun appeared. The camp swarmed with flying ants. Heads still heavy with sleep, we left the barracks and were struck by the size of the destruction from last night's attack. Debris and rocks were everywhere. We spread out our clothes and blankets on tree branches and walls to dry, and then we sat facing the timid sun as we watched swallows chase after the flying ants. I closed my eyes to the sound of my comrades muttering and the sound of birds alighting on the barracks' roofs.

Suddenly, a military march rose up throughout the camp and a voice blared out from the PA system, ordering us to gather in the courtyard. We got dressed in our uniforms (such as they were) and stood amid the mud and water. We batted away the flying ants that grew thicker as soldiers walked toward us and divided us into eight groups, each overseen by an officer. They sat us down in the muddy puddles, and the officers gave a crash course on rifles: breakdown, reassembly, and repairing defects. It wasn't a lengthy explanation, but a rapid one that revealed a boredom borne of having repeated it hundreds of times from memory. Each officer barked a phrase over and over to the conscripts in his group:

– Understand and memorize what I'm going to tell you. Memorize it!

Repeat it to yourself!

Because I am bad at remembering things, I began to scribble the main points of the officer's explanation on my arm. Truth be told, I didn't just write it down; I also drew it out. I sketched a Kalashnikov and indicated its parts with explanatory arrows.

At the end of the lesson, they gave each soldier a metal helmet, a Kalashnikov, and ten shots, which we fired at sandbags set up in front of one of the walls. It wasn't as easy as some had thought. I'm not ashamed to admit that my hands were shaking as I carried a weapon for the first time. The squat soldier who handed me the gun noticed my trembling and bewilderment. He struck a hand against my metal helmet before spitting a profanity at me.

When the sun had risen in the sky to the point where it began to warm our bodies, a raspy voice came over the PA system and ordered us to pack our bags and be ready to depart the camp as soon as possible. We wondered: Where to? The officers' only response was an unending litany of curses. So we wasted no time. The barracks swarmed with chaos and clamour. After we had finished packing, we stood in long lines in the courtyard, our pale faces filled with mixed emotions and thousands of questions on our chapped lips.

The rush of the soldiers betrayed their anxiety. We hurried, too. We wanted all this bullshit to come to an end in any way possible. A soldier with splotchy skin finished reviewing the columns and quickly went over to salute an officer who stood in front of one of the office doors. A few moments later, an officer from the military police stood in front of the formations. He walked between them, examining faces and bodies, casting challenging and provocative glances as he did. When he finished up, he quickly returned to the front of the group. With his hand extended, he pointed toward an open gate and said, in a raised voice:

– Forward, march! Forward, march! Keep in line. Forward!

Military marches trumpeted once more. Several soldiers ran toward us and began roughing us up terribly, one after the other as they repeated:

– Forward, march! Forward!

Do you know what my mind drifted back to as I watched them fall upon person after person? I remembered my mother's fingers as she thumbed through the beads of her *misbaha* in the early morning, each one making a snapping sound. My entire soul filled with the scent of rosemary and her morning coffee. I heard the crowing of our only rooster and the mutterings of my father that he had, somehow, extricated with great difficulty from behind the cruel wall of silence. I also recalled the Eid sheep and the butcher's hand dispatching one right after the other with the glint of the blade and splattering of blood on the tiled floor and onto his high rubber boots.

We departed the camp like an army of ants, walking in a long, silent formation led by a member of the military police. We crossed fields as the sun crossed over us. Young boys secretly peeked at us from behind corn stalks. Farmers refrained from spewing curses this time, and instead shot long depressed glances at us. Out of nowhere came a column of laughing children. They kept running alongside us, panting and teasing.

Unlike the others, I was sullen and silent. I felt as if a noose had been coiled around my neck. Every step forward cinched it more tightly. Fear of the unknown paralyzed my ability to think and almost laid me low. Peering eyes, pitying glances, and flowers' thorns all tried to latch onto our clothes and limbs as we passed by. With no success, they tried to keep us from walking toward our total destruction, toward certain death. Toward a grave somewhere off in the distance whose maw gaped wide open. The few birds that hovered silently in the sky wept for us. Yes, I felt they wept for us.

No creature can imagine the amount of pain eating away at a man who realises he is being driven to his doom. Nor the amount of helplessness that squeezes the body, mind, and soul of a fellow human being as he watches another driven like a lamb to the slaughter. Compassionate glances and pity can be as painful as looks of ridicule and contempt. Both kill a man's pride and reduce his life to nothing more than a repulsive, meaningless mess.

Far off in the distance, from behind the mountain, a military helicopter appeared. When it was over our column, the pilot lowered it down, and the wind from the blades slapped our faces, almost bowling over our emaciated bodies. Children's screams rose in delight at its descent, and they broke through our formation, hiding among the corn stalks and chasing after the helicopter that had disappeared off into the distance.

When we reached the tarmacked road, we found eleven armoured military trucks waiting for us and a dozen and a half from the military police. Over the next half hour, we were randomly divided among the trucks in an arrangement imposed by a man wearing civilian clothes who kept ranting and raving for no reason at all.

When the 12 o'clock hour entered its first seconds, the trucks started to move, and we left the corn fields behind. We also left behind the damp-walled houses and the faces that peered at us. We left behind the eyes that peeped through chinks in the doors and windows. And we left behind the people that stood along the road craning their necks and looking toward us apprehensively. In their eyes, we were mere ewes, forcibly driven to the knife of a butcher for whom mercy found no pathway to his heart, who chopped off heads without batting an eyelash. What pained everyone was that these lambs knew where they were being led and the fate that awaited them.

I stood up and looked all around. A flood of tears welled in my eyes while a volcano erupted inside of me, ejecting bitter lumps that got caught in my dry throat, like a heavy oil slick that stopped me from breathing. I opened my mouth and began to gulp in as much air as I could. I had to swallow the lump and extinguish the log burning inside of me. I almost suffocated from the crying, the tears, the mountain of pain and anguish, and the glances of pity spat into my face. I almost suffocated from the air. Yes, asphyxiated by the air so heavy and pestilent it had become like a pharaonic tomb.

I let my body collapse into a sitting position as I wrestled with my pain and suffocation. Deep within my heart, I wished they had transported us in a truck covered with a tarp. That would have given us at least a more comforting memory of the world we were departing and would have protected us from the prick of merciful glances and the pity that stung us on all sides.

The trucks kept making their way through the streets of the ramshackle town. One long column. Fluttering flags and bullhorns were attached to the cab of each truck. The sky resonated with zealous anthems and military music while the roadways were devoid of vehicles, having been emptied by local police cars that led the column. Like irritated hornets or ravenous locusts, helicopters buzzed above us, coming and going. They were libidinous bees searching for a lost mate or genies consumed by insomnia.

Outside the city...

About twenty kilometres out, at a four-way intersection, the trucks stopped in the fields beside the road. We piled out, carrying our bags, and waited in formation under the heat of the sun for a half hour. The high-strung man wearing civilian clothes came up in an armoured vehicle. He redistributed people across the trucks in a new random order. I mounted the one assigned to me, and Suleiman and others followed my lead. Once the trucks filled up, they departed, splitting off down the four roads, according to a signal given from the military policeman standing at the intersection.

We moved northward in a three-truck convoy along a pitted asphalt road that cut through endless agricultural fields. Infused with the scent of soil, trees, and shrubs, the crispness of January brushed lightly against us. Shepherds drove their flocks to pasture beyond hills that varied in colour from green to flaming yellow, and we caught snatches of peasant folk tunes as we were immersed in the smell of bread baked by their wives in wood ovens.

There were only two clouds in the sky. The wind began to fashion one into the shape of a frowning face that resembled the town mayor. As for the other, the breeze scattered it like the smoke of a recently departed train, while a lazy flock of long-necked migratory birds from the east followed it along in the sky.

I was on board the second truck with Suleiman and thirty others. The sun gently caressed my right side. From my seat, I could see only the faces and bodies that surrounded me—sallow faces oozing fear—and above us nothing but sky and sun. Words withered in our chests and eyes roved all around. How could it be otherwise? The unknown awaited us. Its shadowy maw gaped in our faces, behind which stood a thousand and one possibilities.

I looked at the limp bodies and faces of the lifeless ones in front of me. I didn't know where we were or how far along the route we had come or what time it was. Even if I did know, what value or meaning did time have in a situation like this? Was its value counted in the number of times I felt pain and pity for myself? Or the number of times that I tried to stop myself from crying? Or how often I spat upon the past or the present? Or the times that I cursed the war machine itself? Or the number of times that someone sitting next to me vomited or burst into tears? I don't know! I don't know! I hoped that this journey would end—that everything would somehow just end.

I cast aside everything except for my bag. I grasped it and laid on the truck bed in the foetal position, my body collapsing under the weight of pain and overcrowding. My head succumbed to the dizziness. I felt my brain boiling and tasted blood rising up into my mouth. It was a nosebleed. I pulled out a piece of cloth from my bag and wet it, then placed it on my nose.

Suddenly, Jalal (the conscript who had cursed Abu Rami) stood up among the crowd and vomited over the side of the truck. He wiped his mouth with the sleeve of his shirt then began staring at faces with the bafflement of a disoriented man. Once the clouds of his perplexity lifted, he smiled and cursed at one of the conscripts, jabbing another with his elbow. He got up and cupped his hands around his mouth and shouted into the sky as loud as he could:

– Abu Rami, damn your father, you asshole.

The distant hills rang out with his voice. Before he could smile with any contentment, the truck passed over a speedbump and gave a violent shake. He tumbled against the others and was met with kicks and gut punches. Frightened, he pulled back, taking refuge behind a pile of bags.

Suleiman guffawed loudly, then got up and grabbed two hoses that ran along the roof of the truck. He used them to help make his way toward the middle, where he stood smoking a cigarette and cracking a few jokes, oblivious to the glances of the sergeant who was with us. One of those sitting next to me had grown tired of Suleiman and his antics and whispered:

– He's definitely drunk!

I ignored his whisper and pulled out my phone. I tried several times to call my mother, but there was no network in the area. I grew tired of trying and decided to write a text and let the network decide when to send it. I opened my messages, picked my mother's name from the list of contacts, and wrote:

"How is everyone? I'm well and miss you all so much. We just departed Istiqbal Camp. God alone knows where we're going. I hope to see you soon. I send my love to everyone."

I clicked "send" and tapped to open the photo album. There were pictures of my mother, my father under his grapevine, and my sisters alongside photos of the workshop, corners of the house, my face in various locations, and samples of plasterwork I had made, all looking back at me. The pictures revived me and filled my chest with an odd comfort that overcame a large part of my pains.

Something strange compelled me to turn on the camera and take a few pictures. Yes, I took pictures of everything around me. The faces—dejected, grimacing, dirty, sweat-covered, and anxious. The sky. The fields. The distant mountains. I flipped the camera around to take a selfie. I saw myself as a different person on the phone screen: emaciated, skinny, covered in dust, and with sunken eyes. I saw the helmet that swallowed up half of my head. I gave myself a forced smile then turned off the phone and put it back into my pocket.

The route grew longer. Suleiman hadn't left his spot and Jalal had started back up with his senseless jabbering and cursing of Abu Rami. The trucks did not stop making noise as they jostled along. The sun was still grilling our heads and dizziness was taking its toll.

At that moment, Suleiman's face transformed into a husk of dust-covered skin. Jalal threw up for the fifth time, taking the wind out of his swearing, and he chucked himself on top of the bags like a dead man. Listlessly, eyes circled from face to face, as if the dead were gazing at the dead.

Suddenly, the trucks slowed down and made a sharp turn, causing our bodies to pile up against one another as the drivers veered onto a road that rose up between two mountains. Gear shifts screeched and the engines lulled. The boulders around us were black and glinted in the sun while patches of grass growing in the crevices appeared unnatural. Crows circled in the sky and reddish-brown monkeys surveilled us from atop the rocks.

A strange uneasiness percolated inside of me, floating to the surface of my skin like cold goosebumps, while dizziness filled my insides with a strong desire to vomit. I pulled my bag tightly against my chest. Someone was talking in a loud voice. Suleiman turned to him and responded as he gestured into the distance:

– Tell your mother—

And before he could finish his sentence, a forceful explosion echoed beneath the truck in front of us, lifting its bumper into the air and ripping apart its cabin. A wave of gravel and scorching air slammed into us, stripping skin, kneading bodies like dough, and piling us one on top of another. Before we realised what was going on, we rammed into the truck that had exploded and, in the next second, the third truck crashed into us as well. Rocks and dirt rained down from above the mountain pass. Smoke and dust covered everything while bodies blended together. Cries of terror began to mount.

Suleiman remained standing in place, terrified and confused. Black dirt coated his stern face, petrifying the smile on his lips. Moments later, the sky had rained down buzzing bullets and fire, striking our bodies, the truck's iron fittings, and our belongings, all at incredible speed. It had left us no chance to escape or seek protection. Suleiman's head exploded, scattering its contents everywhere, like a red mist, before he toppled onto me. I felt his body contract and his muscles convulse. As bullets struck him in the back, I heard the final rattle in his throat. His warm blood covered me up like the grave.

From a gap below his arm, I watched in slow motion as panicked bodies were pounded with dirt and blood, crawling over each other like a ball of struggling worms. I saw terrified eyes and blood-smeared hands with their fingers trembling and outstretched toward the mountains, toward the sky, toward nothing. They waved feebly and in defeat, crying for help and trying to grasp at an imaginary rope dangling from the heights of heaven, swinging between their flailing fingers. Throats gurgled with screams. Blood trickled from orifices and wounds. The bullets didn't care though. They continued to relentlessly criss-cross and arc through the void, falling on their target and leaving in their wake a vapor of red mist, fountains of warm blood, and hands clawing feebly at the air.

I was drowning in a pool of blood. Every crevice in me reeked with the stench of blood and human flesh. One of the soldiers beat the bed of the truck with his fist while screaming incoherently. A barrage of fiery bullets shut him up. Another was on his knees, waving with his hands toward the mountains. Before he could say anything or even wipe the blood from his weakened face and eyes, a gunman positioned himself in the opening of one of the caves that overlooked the road and fired off a heavy round that rocked the bones in his chest and broke his left forearm.

I shut my eyes, embraced my fear, and surrendered, awaiting my fate, my portion of all this bullshit. In an instant, the cries died out while bullets continued to ricochet against the ground and metal. Then everything fell completely still. A few moments of silence followed and, before I could think of anything, it seemed as if the mountain boulders and caves echoed in an overlapping chorus of sounds. The sound of my mother's weeping intermingled with my sisters shouting in grief.

Something strange awoke in me, injecting my veins with a miraculous force. I freed myself from my fear and the weight of Suleiman's body. I crawled between the corpses, the blood, and dismembered body parts. I reached the back of the truck and climbed over the hatch and threw myself outside. Crashing onto the asphalt with a thud, I hid under the truck. A river of blood poured out of the back through the holes, spilling onto the asphalt. I crawled toward the third truck and hid beneath it. Sounds grew closer and boulders rolled down from the top of the slope while bullets whizzed here and there. I only had a few seconds to escape.

I crawled toward the nearest rock. From behind it, in one direction, I could see corpses and chaos. In the other, there was a deep gorge. I glanced between the two scenes and heard the sound of feet treading on gravel. One of them was laughing. Another coughed, and a third one ... The sound of a mercy shot rang out.

I had no other choice. I turned and launched myself into the abyss. For an eternity, my body hung in the void. All sounds vanished as did my sense of time and place. I felt like an astronaut who had lost his way in the vacuum of the space. I nearly smiled. I swear I almost did, but the first signs of my smile disappeared as soon as I slammed violently onto the ground. I rolled down dirt, gravel, rocks, and thorns and came to a rest next to a thicket of cactus and boxthorn.

I crawled to the thicket and shoved my body inside, ignoring the thorns and all the pain that shot through my body. I was trembling with fear and anguish, and I don't know when I lost control of my bladder. I didn't know where to begin or what to do. My ability to think was completely paralyzed. I cried. Yes, I cried like a child all alone, overcome by fright during a dark night.

A clamour rose. Then the sound of intense gunfire echoed. My body shook. I stuck my head out, and I saw those who had survived running aimlessly between boulders, trees, and cacti. Bullets chased them, felling them one by one. I crouched down further in the thicket and held my breath, pushing back my tears. As I put my head between my knees, I closed my eyes. The situation didn't last terribly long. The gunfire stopped and the attackers' voices became lewder and more savage. The sound of sporadic gunfire from a heavy weapon reverberated, and then I heard a voice call out:

– Enough! Enough!

Suddenly, everything went quiet. I heard the sound of a helicopter hovering high above. A few seconds later, the strange cawing of an unseen crow masked the noise, and a black curtain of smoke dropped over the scene.

This moment of respite lasted only a few minutes. Afterward, I heard something like the sound of heavy objects being tossed from atop the slope. Oh my God. Had the attackers decided to inspect the slope? I gathered up what remained of my courage and tried to see what was going on. Before I could get anywhere, something heavy slid down and came to a rest just steps away from me, kicking up a cloud of dust as it did. When it had dispersed, I saw a corpse crumpled up and covered in blood laying in front of me. Its limbs were twisted in a sickening way. For a few seconds, I sat there staring at it, terrified and unable to absorb the situation. I retreated, panic-stricken, while I stared at the corpse, the head had been hollowed out from behind like a dinner bowl. It was the body of Suleiman. Those two eyes filled with dirt were his—the traces of horror still visible. I wasn't wrong. I couldn't mistake the structure of his face or the almond shape of his eyes.

The attackers continued to toss down bodies. I saw them tumble over rocks and thorns, body parts twisting as if they were puppets. Something huge crashed inside of me, leaving my heart empty and my eyes open wide in panic. I couldn't stop my limbs from shaking. I don't know how long this went on, but in a moment it stopped, and everything went still.

In spite of the sobbing and fear which continued to erupt inside of me, I gathered my strength and began to pull the thorns from my skin. My eyes didn't stop watching Suleiman's corpse. It gave me the impression that his eyes were fixed on me, observing what I was doing. I thought for a moment that he would speak or call out to me. When I finished removing the thorns, I found myself staring at him, slack-jawed. I saw him blink, and the muscles in his face contracted. Panicked, I froze. I uprooted the grass between my feet and threw it on his face again and again until I had covered it up completely.

Cautiously, I got up, moving my gaze from behind the boxthorn tree toward the top of the slope. Fire was devouring our three trucks. My eyes moved across the peaks and rocky desert terrain. It would be stupid to hope they had left the area already. I would wait. Yes, I would wait until the cover of night fell. Then I would head out to look for an escape from this cursed mess.

I noticed a gold-plated lighter about to fall out of Suleiman's jacket pocket. I don't know what went through my mind, but I grabbed a dry branch and carefully removed it. I pulled it toward me and flipped it upside down before putting it in my pocket.

Time moved slowly. Heavily. Sleep finally overtook me, but a grasshopper pouncing on my face pulled me right out of it. I found myself on the edge of nightfall. Before night could lower its veil, I killed a large scorpion that was crawling on my left thigh. I took off my helmet and placed it over Suleiman's face like a cover. I said my goodbyes, then walked hunched over between the plants and rocks, heading toward the valley.

Darkness overtook me before I could make it to the valley. I tripped several times and thorns burrowed painfully into my body. When I had reached the valley, I ran the first hundred metres then stopped and looked back to where the mountainous heights rose like a dark black mass against the background of a sky embroidered with stars. I took two steps over the branches of a banana tree until I could see the tongues of flames still licking at the three trucks, illuminating the mountain pass with an orange glow. I went back to walking, feeling my way in the dark through the mud, encircled by thorns on all sides. At one point, I heard what sounded like a water pump coming from somewhere off in the dark. I made a beeline for it. I crossed a thorny fence and immediately found myself in front of the pump.

I inspected the area carefully. When I confirmed that it was completely empty, I approached the water that was flowing swiftly into the canal. I cupped my hands and took a sip. I laid down on the ground and covered my face with water, drinking from it until I was quenched. I got up and pulled my belongings from my clothes, dropping them onto the ground, and threw my body into the irrigation canal. The water was warm. I grabbed the edge of the canal to fight the torrential current then heaved myself out to lay on the ground, staring mindlessly at the sky. A long time passed with me in that state. Cold and drowsiness began to seep into my body. Before my mind could plunge into the abyss of unconsciousness, I heard dogs barking off in the distance. Alert and frightened, I quickly got up and gathered my things from the ground and put them into my pocket. Darkness wiped across my eyes, and everything appeared calm. Even the barking had stopped. Yet this didn't mean everything was going to be alright. I was still in the crosshairs, and I had to do whatever I could to get away from that place. I got up and started walking again.

All the fields and trails were empty. Only stray dogs and night insects broke through the virginal stillness of the heavy silence. Weariness overtook me, so I stretched out on the roof of a dark building annexed to one of the farms, staring into the sky and chewing some of the vegetables I had gathered from the fields. I watched the flames in the mountain pass—they had now become a very small speck—and I watched as rounds of bright bullets whizzed through the valley in zigzagging lines. Their sound traversed the whole area, then trailed off as they reached me, like a weak clinking echo from the depths of a bottomless well.

Chapter 11

The Family of Muhi Al-Deen Al-Niqash

January 5

The third day

Early that morning...

After my mother had performed her *fajr* prayer, she began to inspect the house. She found bullets had broken all the windows and lodged into the walls of the sitting area and bedrooms, ruining the furniture and destroying the carpets that hung on the walls.

Neighbours came to the house in throngs and offered their help as they tried to figure out what had happened. My mother didn't know what to say. There was no hostility between us or anyone, nor did we have money that assailants would greedily covet. That is exactly what my mother told the police officer who came that morning to investigate, accompanied by the mayor, and who had left without jotting a single thing down in his notebook. The mayor appeared paler in that moment than he ever had before.

One of the neighbours told my mother that they had found thirty-five bullets in the house. After everyone had disbanded, my mother gathered my sisters and some women from the neighbourhood and swept the house, taking the carpets down, and collecting the rubble in big plastic sacks. She then mixed a bucket of plaster and filled in the holes in the wall.

By the time the men had finished repairing the windows and installing a new water tank on the roof, the muezzin announced over the loudspeaker that the mayor had suddenly passed away. The news struck everyone like a bolt of lightning. My mother beat her chest in grief and wept when she thought of him standing in front of her just hours before. The men departed, heading toward the mosque to attend the funeral prayer, while my mother closed the door of our house and went to the mayor's home to offer her condolences.

As the afternoon call to prayer sounded, she left to collect her food rations. She was surprised when a heavyset worker with a thick coastal accent informed her that her name wasn't on the list. She tried to explain and to get help, but she couldn't find anyone who would listen or assist her, and she could do nothing other than leave and return home under the assault of an unexpected downpour.

She neared the house in soaking clothes, her hands shivering, and her breathing shallow and rapid. She sat in a nearby corner and asked for her coffee in a soft voice. Her cup sat in front of her, untouched. Not saying a word, she just stared at her coffee in silence. In one night, my mother had grown old, appearing as if she had aged a decade. Nobody had ever seen her in such a weakened and pallid state. Tears hung heavily in my sisters' eyes. One of them brought over a tray with dates and placed it in front of her. The others ate them up, despite her protests. In an instant, she raised her coffee cup and took a long sip from it, which brightened her face. Meanwhile, my father was sitting in the family room, staring into space. Without moving his eyes, which were fixed on the floor, or making the slightest expression, he said:

– Forty-five years ago on a Tuesday afternoon, four seagulls landed on the minaret of the mosque. Not two or three, but four seagulls. No one knew how they had traversed such a distance that separated our town from the nearest sea, and the villagers considered it a bad omen for the town. A Jewish shoemaker based his interpretation on the principle of "like for like". He explained that a flood would inundate the town. He didn't say "flood" exactly, but he did say the town would turn into a sea. Nobody believed him, because there was no river or sea nearby and the rainy season had not yet begun.

Five days after this prophecy and precisely in the afternoon of the fifth day, the inhabitants of the village heard a terrifying clatter that sounded like a dozen tree trunks crashing down. When they came out of their houses to see what was going on, they saw a huge cloud of dust obscuring the horizon. A cold wind, filled with the scent of water, blew in their faces. Minutes of alarm passed, followed by a violent deluge that swept away everything in its path. The whole situation lasted no more than an hour, but, in its wake, the flood left houses and streets under tons of mud and rubble. The men of the village who survived, along with men from neighbouring towns, worked tirelessly to clear the village and its houses of corpses, mud, and rubble. They shovelled the mud with everything they could find and carried it away in donkey carts to the outskirts of town. There, they piled it up into a huge heap on fallow land that had never been cultivated. For some unknown reason, they then dug forty-eight graves into the mud of this hill for those who had perished in the catastrophe, and they erected grave markers made of red calcite stone. Despite the long years that have passed, not a single blade of grass has grown on the dirt of that hill, which remains barren like the ground it was heaped onto.

When the men reached the shoemaker's house, they found it filled to the rafters with mud. The men spent three days clearing the house of mud and the corpses of the shoemaker, his wife, and eight children. On the morning of the fourth day, the rabbi from the capital came to collect the bodies that had been wrapped in blankets. Two hours after the rabbi had left, the men heard the crying of an infant coming from the shoemaker's house. They looked around, befuddled. The men were hesitant to enter the house because it had been rumoured that the man's wife dabbled in magic, and they thought perhaps the crying was nothing more than one of her evil spirits toying with them or warning them against coming any closer.

The men were increasingly racked with uncertainty and panic. When the infant's crying grew louder, three of the men volunteered to enter the house and investigate the situation. They were startled to find an infant in the fireplace covered in mud and soot. One of them grabbed him and wiped his face with a wet rag and took him out. Faces soiled with mud and eyes filled with concern gathered in a circle around him. Opinions clashed over his identity. Some confirmed he was indeed the son of the Jewish shoemaker, citing the fact that his nose resembled his father's. Others said that the shoemaker didn't have an infant, and they thought it likely that the flood had brought him here from somewhere else. After all, it had left in its wake dozens lost among the towns and villages. After some back and forth, opinion finally settled on presenting the infant in the town mosque and making the rounds with him to mosques in the neighbouring villages, too. Perhaps the news would reach the ears of his family.

The men visited the mosques of each town and hamlet in the flood's path and showed them the infant, but had no luck finding his parents. They returned the way they had come, carrying their confusion and the infant who would not stop crying.

The village's inhabitants gathered in the mosque and placed the crying baby, wrapped in a rough linen diaper, under the dome of the mosque. One of them had a modicum of religious training and held the baby in his hands, telling them that he was born in his "natural state," that is to say as a Muslim (disregarding the conclusive proof that he was the son of the Jewish cobbler), and therefore it was not permissible to give him up to the rabbi. Rather it was necessary to give him a Muslim name and raise him among themselves. Nobody objected, and they chose a compound name: Naji-Awad, pronounced with no division in between the names. "Naji" because God had saved him from this catastrophe and "Awad" for the person who had retrieved him from the cobbler's hearth. The men of the village approved of the name, or so they feigned. In reality, they just wanted to be done with this whole infant situation any which way they could. Suddenly, the man passed the crying infant in front of everyone and asked:

– Who wants to adopt him, for God's sake?

Eyes locked. Lips and faces froze. When he received no response, he nestled him against his chest and said, smiling:

– I will adopt him for God's sake!

As soon as he finished talking, the infant stopped crying. The infant began to gaze intently at the men's faces with eyes that, according to one of them present, were not the eyes of a baby. He recalled those eyes a quarter of a century later, shortly before he passed away from dysentery.

Naji Awad spent his childhood and a large part of his adolescence in the home of his adoptive father. When he finished his studies, he joined the police college. During his last year in college, his adoptive father died, ripping the family apart to such an extent that even the memory of it disappeared. All that remained was the rundown house, over which distant relatives vied for ownership. In the same year and because of his Jewish roots, which nobody knew how the authorities had come to know, he was transferred to the Political Guidance Committee instead of performing security work.

Up until that point, people had forgotten the whole affair of the infant, the flood, and the shoemaker and even the whole story of the barren hill with its red calcite gravestones. However, the news of Naji Awad's transfer to Political Guidance and the fraying of his adoptive family revived the story in the minds of a minority of elderly people who were still alive and had lived through it. Naturally, because of the numerous narrators and many years that had come and gone, there were those who added to the story and some who invented a new story that had nothing to do with the original at all, even though the "true story" itself was predicated on supposition and not actual knowledge.

Confronted with losing the job he had dreamed of and the whispering and furtive eyes that enveloped him, Naji Awad had to surrender to this fate that life had unexpectedly revealed. Feelings of being cheated and wronged began to grow inside him unchecked. He felt lonely and longed for a family to reunite the breakup of his own. This combination of feelings transformed into a tempestuous flood of anger and vengeance, especially after the revelation of his Jewish roots.

Following the silver anniversary of the security forces, one of the intelligence agents submitted a report to the authorities, confirming that he had seen Naji Awad in the capital's Jewish quarter several times. Truth be told, Naji Awad was not innocent of these charges. He also wasn't guilty. He used to frequent the Jewish neighbourhood, searching for any lead at all that would steer him to the rabbi who had received the bodies of his family members and perhaps find a way to access the Jewish community's records to learn more about them and see their place of burial. He was ready to do anything to settle the issue once and for all, including DNA tests. To be more precise, Naji Awad needed to satiate his desire to belong, especially after his community had stepped away from him after his backstory had come out. Unfortunately, the authorities didn't view his behaviour through this lens, and he was arrested and thrown into prison, where the investigators humiliated him, degraded his humanity, and broke his pride. During this period, every ideal and value inside of him turned to shit, giving birth to a ferocious monster inside him that kept growing and waiting for the opportunity to come out.

Eight and a half months later, Naji Awad was released. After proving his innocence of even a hint of anti-revolutionary involvement or conspiring with Jewish organizations to resettle Jews in Palestine, he left prison. He remained out of work for a year and a half.

This period was the hinge point in his life. He learned all the vices of the world while working as a dealer at gambling tables in various nightclubs before returning to his career, for which he was transferred to work in one of the large prisons on the coast. There, he spent a year and a half and married one of the female inmates. He grew bored of the work and applied to be transferred to his hometown. When notice of his acceptance arrived, he took his wife and returned to the shoemaker's house, which had been abandoned since the flood. Shrubs had grown inside it, on its roof and along the mud walls. Naji Awad demolished it and built a large, new house on the ruins and settled down.

After my father had finished narrating his story, he went off to bed.

That night, my mother wept in her sleep, letting out heavy sighs made thicker by her tears. Her sighs woke my father from the depths of his slumber and left him staring absentmindedly at the ceiling, tears pouring from his own eyes. He wasn't the only one torn apart by sorrow. On the other side of the wall, sadness and weeping crushed the three girls.

Somehow, members of the family realised, each in their own way, that sorrow and pain had descended on the house ever since I had gone to the front. Yet they were expecting something still worse, so they continued to downplay what was happening and to underestimate its importance even if it was formidable, which made the even more difficult events in the coming days easier to handle.

Suddenly, in that moment of pain, the sound of a plane circling over the town drew close. It was sharp and piercing. Some even thought the jet was directly over their roofs.

My older sister got up quickly and opened the doors and windows, ready for anything, and ready to activate the emergency instructions that the local PA system had repeated day and night during the first year of war. My mother awoke in a panic and carried my father to the sitting room, where the girls gathered around him. In an instant, everyone heard a sharp, ear-splitting whistle. Their necks craned, and they held their breath. Then a large explosion echoed. Doors slammed shut and my father's sculptures tumbled off the shelves while pictures fell off the wall, smashed to pieces. The joints of the walls creaked, and the house was filled with screams, dust, and the smell of gunpowder.

During these difficult moments, my mother prayed to God while holding on as tight as she could to the girls, who did not stop screaming. My father alone remained frozen. This time, he did not scream.

When the jet left our airspace, my mother discovered that my youngest sister was missing. She screamed in grief and started yelling her name in panic. She looked for her in the bedrooms and kitchen. When she didn't find her, she opened the house's front door and ran into the courtyard, then barefoot toward the street. The air was redolent with the smell of gunpowder and charred flesh. Screaming and wailing resounded in the sky and the alleys of the town. My sister Hinaa called out, and my mother stopped in the middle of the courtyard and turned toward her like a madwoman. My sister said immediately:

– She's here! Inside!

My mother turned around and came back, plodding and faltering as she did. When she found her sitting in a corner of the bathroom shaking like a wet pigeon, she threw her body on top of her. She hugged her and began kissing her, crying louder than she had never cried before. After she regained her composure, she moistened her with water and carried her to the sitting room. Since then, that corner has become a refuge for my youngest sister whenever fear has gotten the best of her.

Chapter 12

Naji Awad

January 5

The third day

The mayor woke up after the sun had risen. His young wife Reem, who was still in her twenties, was not by his side. She was in the kitchen with the rest of the women of the house. As he laid there staring into the void, Reem opened the bedroom door and placed breakfast on the bed. She feigned a smile. He returned it with one even more pale than the face of the dead. He didn't hear her mumble. He was distracted by the details of her voluptuous body. Often, he wished that time would go back ten years. Just ten. Things would definitely have been different, the pleasures of life more radiant.

She left him and closed the bedroom door behind her. He pulled open one of the nightstand's drawers and took out a small glass jar. He opened the lid with his trembling hand began to dip his fingers in the contents, licking them until he was sated. He closed it and put it back in the drawer. He pulled the breakfast tray over and began to sip his tea with honey, which his first wife, Mehdiya, had masterfully prepared for him. Nobody could rival her. He was unable, however, to take even one bite. He felt palpitations in his chest. Placing a pill under his tongue, he grabbed his phone and dialled Naji Awad's number. The phone kept ringing. No response at all. At that very moment, Naji Awad was still fully asleep and half naked. He wasn't sleeping in his house, but was sprawled out on a luxurious bed in a room on the third floor of a newly built home in the suburbs, owned by one of his pimp friends.

Naji Awad woke up at midday. Nothing covered his private parts save an embroidered linen bedsheet. His eyes roved over the sophisticated furniture and erotic paintings hanging on the walls and the bottles discarded on the floor. It was a few moments before he fully regained his senses and balance and realised where he was.

He got up and made his way toward the bathroom naked. On the wash-basin, he saw the two devices that he had bought from the pimp. He took one and began to inspect it closely. In his opinion, the device was nothing more than a useless plastic tube. He sensed deep within him that that pimp had sold him a load of horseshit. He chucked both devices into the waste-basket and said, in a rage:

– Fucking bitch.

He stood under the flow of water and closed his eyes in surrender. Re-vived once more, he wrapped a towel around his lower half and went into the room where he sat on the edge of the bed. There, he pulled a cigarette from the pocket of his shirt, which had been tossed on the floor. Licking it, he placed it in his mouth and lit it. He searched through his phone's contact list. He muttered:

– Eight missed calls? What does this guy want?

He dialled the number and waited until the mayor responded in an agi-tated whisper:

– Where are you?!

– I was sleeping. What do you want?

– What you did to the Al-Niqash residence, I don't...

He interrupted sharply:

– I didn't do anything. What happened to them?

He heard a long sigh on the other end of the line, then an angry voice:

– You know exactly what happened. Everybody knows that you're the one who did it. I advise you to put an end to this insanity.

He interrupted, even more agitated:

– You're advising me or you're threatening me?

– ...

He heard the phone go dead on the other end. He flew into a rage, his eyes darting around the room. Then he chucked the phone against the opposite wall, smashing it into pieces. At that moment, his female companion walked up, wearing a robe befitting her profession. She came closer, trying to soothe and caress him, but he cursed and pushed her roughly to the side. He made his way over to the closet and quickly got dressed. In the street, he discovered that he had forgotten his gun and hurried back. Twenty devils were spinning in his head. He grabbed his gun from under the pillow and left.

Parked in front of his house, he saw the car of a hairdresser. He remembered that his wife was busy preparing a bride, which granted him momentary relief from his headache.

He entered the house through the back door. The house was booming with wedding songs and overflowed with the smell of cosmetics and women's muttering. He changed his clothes and headed out to the police station.

He walked into his office and closed the door. He ordered coffee then tea, made a few calls, and went on smoking. When he felt capable of controlling the situation, he phoned the mayor. He spoke with him gently, then invited him to his office to have a cup of coffee. The mayor accepted his invitation and hung up. Although he didn't drink alcohol during the day, he felt an urgent need for it. He pulled a bottle from his desk drawer and took a long sip then put it back. He burped, took out another cigarette, and lit it.

***

Twenty years ago, he had learned about the theory of "extracting nails." Not the nails you might think of, but those that are driven into your head and into the depths of your heart, continuously driving interminable pain into your soul, depriving you of sleep and obstructing the very course of your life. Some people resorted to various methods to get rid of these nails. But due to their sheer number, it would require an inordinate amount of time and effort, and, if the nail you were dealing with was particularly tricky, you might not be successful.

One day, the fates ordained that a transient old man would be Naji Awad's teacher. In a previous life, this teacher had been an incomparable painter. But years of depression and stagnant art markets left him to trawling bars and nightclubs, where he first noticed Naji Awad, distracted, at a table in a club. He went up and took a seat across from him. Then, with the eloquence of a mystic well-versed in the art of probing a man's depths, he said:

– Why don't you extract the nail that is bothering you and be done with it, all in the blink of an eye? Save yourself from the trouble of waiting and pain!

The old man's words illuminated something deep inside Naji Awad. He stared at the face of this old man, who kept talking nonstop, even though he was no longer listening. Instead, he was analysing the theory, interpreting it, and transforming it into a workable program. Suddenly, he got up and left the bar, leaving behind the old man at the table, still rambling on about the injustice of people and the tyranny of fate. That night, Naji Awad pulled out the first nail in his life. Ever since, Naji Awad had been a zealous proponent of this theory. Testing it out, he found that it eliminated burdensome weights from his mind and life.

***

In his intoxicated state, he thought about the old man who had invented the theory and arrived at the conclusion that he deserved the Nobel Prize for science and humanity. Why not? It brought about what the medicine of doctors and wisdom of sages couldn't.

While waiting for the mayor, he made several phone calls and had a quick breakfast with several cups of coffee. He had begun to smoke like a chimney when there was a knock on his office door. Feebly, the mayor approached, encircled by a large cloud of cigarette smoke. He coughed several times then said, weakly:

– What's with all this smoke?

Naji Awad didn't stand up when he entered, as he had done before. Rather, he greeted him and, with the blade of a letter opener, pointed toward the chair. The mayor sat down then asked, drily:

– Why did you call for me?

– Everything is fine!

The mayor took a piece of paper from the surface of the desk and began to fan his face, saying:

– Be straight with me, give me what you've got.

– What makes you think I'm the one who assaulted the Al-Niqash home?

The mayor smiled wryly, then said:

– Don't forget that not a single person has tossed even a pebble at the Al-Niqash home, at least since I've come to this town. And also, don't forget that I went to the Al-Niqash home and talked to them about their daughter. And don't forget that what happened occurred *after* your request for their daughter was refused!

A coughing fit seized him. He took out his handkerchief and spat into it. He caught his breath and said in weak warning, while pointing his trembling finger:

– Nobody in this town has a strong motivation to harm the Al-Niqash family except you.

The mayor took a breath, then continued, his voice trembling:

– I know you like the back of my hand. Not just me, but everyone else in the town, too. What you're doing is not hidden from anyone!

Naji Awad was stunned. The mayor had never spoken to him in this manner before. He began to speak. However, another coughing fit attacked him. He took out an inhaler, placed it in his mouth for a few seconds, then returned it to his pocket. The mayor felt that he had been frank, much as he dealt with all people, but decided to give Naji Awad a margin to manoeuvre. He caught his breath and said:

– If it wasn't you, then it was someone on your side or someone who wants to pin it on you.

Naji Awad listened to him while cleaning his fingernails with the letter opener. When he heard the mayor's final words, a strange smile etched across his face. Then he got up from behind his desk and moved toward the window, gazing outside. The mayor's gentle voice came to him, advising him:

– You have to moderate your behaviour. The Al-Niqash family is weak. Harming them will only bring about your damnation!

He cut off his phrase suddenly and disappeared into a torrent of coughing. Naji Awad lit a cigarette, then stretched out his hand to lower the blinds. He walked calmly toward the door, locking it. He returned to the mayor and said:

– You treat me unfairly, Mayor. I had no hand in what happened. It could easily be an anomaly. You know, because of the war, weapons are within everyone's reach and events like this are happening everywhere.

At that moment, the mayor finished dosing himself with another puff. Then he said, in a trembling voice:

– Why did you shut the door? I'm suffocating!

Naji Awad stood directly behind him, then took out his handkerchief and placed it into the palm of his hand. Gritting each letter through his teeth, he said:

– Okay, mayor. I'm the one who shot up the Al-Niqash house. And I'm the one who killed the metalworker, Yahya Al-Rumi. And I'll tell you something even more infuriating: I'm the one who harassed your beautiful wife and fondled her on more than one occasion. That mole planted on her chin and her firm body really turn me on!

He placed his hands on the mayor's shoulders and added:

– I'm jealous of you, mayor. And my mind won't be at ease until I have her. But you, alas, will not possess her at all. Do you know why?

The mayor's face clouded over, and he coughed out the medicine in his chest. Before he could even say a word, Naji Awad swooped down on him, handkerchief in hand, and cut off his breath while viciously saying:

– Because you won't be around. Go to hell with your secrets and torments. From down there, you'll see me and what I'm going to do with your beautiful girl.

He pressed down on the mayor's nose and mouth with all the hate he could muster. He squeezed mercilessly on those two lips which had kissed hers and ignited his imagination. This took no more than five seconds, before the body of the mayor went limp forever.

***

After sunset, Naji Awad found himself sitting with the police crew, drinking bitter coffee in the mayor's funeral tent. His clan had come quickly from the countryside and erected it in front of the mayor's home. The place was crowded, and talk revolved around his virtuous qualities and his sudden fatal heart attack.

He didn't feel the slightest sting of conscience. He was positive that the mayor had gotten his share of worldly pleasure, the likes of which others in this town had never had. And for that reason alone, the decision to send him off into a final retirement was the right decision, taken at the right time, so that Naji Awad too could relax like the mayor!

In that moment, he became suffocated by faces and muttering, and noticed his bladder had swelled. He left the tent and went toward the restroom that was in the courtyard behind the mayor's house. He crossed a long dark alley and, when he approached the toilet, he was hit with the pungent stench of ammonia. He closed the door and sat on the toilet. He emptied his bladder, then took out a cigarette and lit it. Clearing his throat, he pulled out a small flask of alcohol from inside his vest and downed half of it in a single gulp. He then returned it to the vest pocket and continued smoking.

He heard muttering and women's voices growing louder only to trail off. He tossed his cigarette to the side and got up from the toilet, then pulled up his pants and zipped them up. Before he could wash his hands, he heard a woman's voice that aroused all his senses. It disappeared, then returned a few seconds later. He had no doubt at all that it was Reem's. To reach the window that looked out onto another open window and into the mayor's home, he placed a bucket below the window and turned off the light. He saw Reem and Mahdiya and a crowd of women. He peered intently at her face. He could tell that it was sad, depressed, wan, and full of brown freckles. He saw women in a state he had never seen before in his life. No beauty, no allure—only a despondent sadness swept across their faces. He felt something strange possess him. He got down from the window and turned on the light, then washed his hands and face.

He came out of the restroom and stood in front of the door, breathing in the night air. He raised his eyes toward the sky. He felt that he could no longer bear his sorrows and considered leaving the tent and going to his nightly gathering.

Just then, his phone rang. He stared at the screen for several seconds before he answered. The caller was speaking quickly and tensely, informing him that the army had confiscated the arms shipment. His face darkened. He was shaken to the core. The caller also told him that military intelligence was onto him and insisted that he go into hiding. When Naji Awad heard all this, his throat went dry. His strength failed him, and he sat on the ground. Recovering himself, he asked the caller if everything he said had been confirmed. The caller chided and cursed him, then hung up. He continued to stare at the ground in terror for several moments. Then, raising his phone, he began to dial a few numbers. Nobody picked up. He thought for a while, then made another call. After a short hesitation, an automated voice responded, speaking in French. He closed the phone and stood up.

The world was crashing in on him. He was suffocating.

At that moment, the sound of a fighter jet circling in the sky above the town reached his ears. The sound was high and piercing. And before he could take one step, he heard a sharp whistle. He knew the sound well, but he wasn't able to grasp the situation. He froze in place, his eyes fixated on nothing. Suddenly, a red flash crashed into the tent and a hot wave of flaming air blew into his face, knocking him off his feet and launching him several feet back. His body slammed against a wall, then dropped onto the ground. He breathed in dirt. The sound in his ears morphed into sharp whistling. He tried to move, but his body failed him, and he was flooded by numbness. The taste of blood and gunpowder swelled inside of him. Before he could shut his eyes, he saw a violent fire break out in the place where the tent had been set up and in the windows of the house that overlooked it.

The town shook to the rhythm of the shelling. People were terrified. They fled their homes, stunned and frightened. The sky over the town was filled with screaming and smoke and the smell of charred flesh. It didn't take long for them to realise that a jet had bombed the mayor's funeral tent, resulting in a large number of dead and injured and devastating the surrounding homes. The town's men and boys brought water canisters and began to put out the fires. Others removed corpses and transported the injured to the town hospital, which was not equipped to handle a catastrophe of this magnitude. The hospital's twenty beds were soon filled. When the ambulance brought more injured to the hospital, the beds of those with light to medium injuries were evacuated and transferred to the hospital's courtyard. They were placed anywhere that was suitable: under trees, under the stairs, behind the main gate, inside the guard shack. It soon became a fracas of crying, moaning, and screaming.

Under a cypress tree in the hospital courtyard, a corpse was placed on the tile without a sheet. Nobody paid much attention to this body, the flesh of which had been singed off by fire, along with most of his clothing. It was left to stare blankly at the sky with two frozen eyes, as if God had made them without eyelids. Feet stepped over it. One of the first responders approached quickly and took its pulse. He found no trace of life. He got up and called to someone and pointed at the dead body, saying:

– Put them here!

Men brought over corpses of those who were killed, still wrapped in whatever they'd been carried in. Bodies were piled over and beside the corpse until it vanished under a heap of charred bodies.

Movement in the hospital didn't slow, nor did the screams of pain in its corridors dissipate. The hospital crew and volunteers felt impotent in the face of this catastrophe. Sedatives ran out, as did bandages. Doctors improvised. They washed wounds with saline solution and improvised pain relief with injections of paracetamol. A single IV pack was used for several injured and had to alternate among them. Hospital staff tore curtains and bedsheets and used them to bandage wounds and used blankets as gurneys. The imam of the new mosque urged people via loudspeaker to donate blood. Doctors fought back exhaustion and the feeling of impotence in the hope that aid would arrive from the Ministry of Emergencies.

In the middle of all that, and while everyone was distracted, one of the piled-up bodies under the cypress tree rolled down, followed by another and another, allowing a disfigured Naji Awad to emerge from among all the corpses. He moaned and vomited a large inky mass, wiped his mouth, and looked around the room in a daze. He crawled on his knees toward a dark

corner and, with trembling fingers, he felt his face and neck. His mind recalled everything that had happened, and he remembered how he had become a target of the army and was currently a wanted man.

He got up gingerly. He walked feebly along the perimeter of the hospital.
Arriving at the rear patio, he climbed with great difficulty onto the barri-
er and then heaved himself outside the hospital. He gathered himself and
walked through the darkened alleys. He ignored his pains and the smell of
burnt flesh that swelled within him. At this pivotal moment of his life, he
did not want anyone to know that he was still alive—even his wife Fathiya—at least for now. When he had saved himself and settled down in a se-
cure location, then he would send for her.

He went to his house and walked around it to confirm that nobody was
watching him. The house was unusually dark on all four sides. Fathiya must
be searching for him now, or at least joining the women of the town to help
with the injured.

He entered the house through the back door. He headed toward the
bathroom and closed the door behind him. He stood in front of the mirror.
Seeing himself in that state horrified him. Most of the hair on his face and
head had been singed off, and what was left was covered in a layer of dried
blood and caked-on dirt. As for his skin, it was as if it had been flayed and
peeled off. The little that remained was black.

Taking off his torn clothes was agonizing, and he reached for a bottle of
vodka from the fridge before sitting on a chair next to the mirror. After he
gulped down several swigs and got ahold of himself, he placed a handkerchief in his mouth and poured the vodka on his wounds. He suppressed a
scream that almost escaped, then washed his skin with a rag, rubbing most
of it over and over but without much effect. Finally, he took hair clippers
and shaved the little hair that remained on his head and upper lip.

When finished, he stood panting and staring at his new self in the mirror. It was as if he were staring at someone completely and totally different. In spite of his physical and mental pain, he was sure that his new look would conceal him from everyone's eyes. However, before escaping and before anything else, he had to get some medical assistance. The only one he could trust in the world was Antar. He exited the bathroom, went toward his bedroom, and closed the door behind him. Sitting on the side of his bed, he grabbed his address book and began flipping through its pages, stopping at one of them. He lifted the phone's receiver and began to dial the numbers. However, he stopped when he heard his wife's voice. He was taken aback by her presence in the house. He began to hang up the phone, but he stopped when he heard her say:

– They say he was killed! I'm sure of it. They found his mobile at the site of the explosion.

A man asked:

– Did they find his body?

All his senses awoke. He heard her reply:

– No. It was probably shredded.

– ...

– But I'm positive he was there. Even if he had survived, the intelligence services and army are looking for him, and they won't rest until they throw him into the most wretched prison in the country.

– My darling. Please don't be hasty. Let's see what happens tomorrow.

– But...

– But what? We can't destroy everything that we built in one moment. Tomorrow everything will come to light, and we will see what we will do. Everything in due time.

He removed the phone from his ear, letting it dangle toward the floor. He looked down in bewilderment as his wife's voice still echoed from the phone receiver. For the first time in his life, his heart crumbled. His nose filled with mucus, and he picked at it slowly. He regained his composure and carefully put back the receiver. He got up and put on clean clothes and took his revolver from the closet along with two stacks of money. Before he left, he went to the bathroom and collected his old clothes in a plastic sack and tidied the bathroom. He then left the house as surreptitiously as he had entered. He walked under a veil of gloom, avoiding people and main roads. Despite the stench of blood which filled him entirely, he could still smell the gunpowder and fire. In an instant, and before he could hop over a pothole at the end of the dark alley, he heard a high-pitched voice calling him:

– You.

He stopped and drew his gun. When he saw no one, he continued on his way. The voice called him several more times, and each time he would stop and find nobody. When he reached the outskirts of town, the beckoning voice was still pursuing and calling after him. A small fear crept into his heart. He flagged down a taxi. When he got in the back seat, he tossed some folded-up bills at the driver and told him to take him to the neighbouring town. The car sped off and the voice calling out vanished as Naji Awad's mind slipped into a slumber. Static from the radio, however, pulled him back, and he stared out into the blackness. Suddenly, the static morphed into the blurry sound of the radio dial rapidly scanning through stations at random. Voices and topics intersected and overlapped. He felt pain in his head, and he called out sharply to the driver, who was completely wrapped in darkness:

– Shut off the radio!

The driver turned on the overhead light and said, while looking at Naji Awad in the rear-view mirror:

– Excuse me, did you say something to me?

Without responding, Naji Awad moved his eyes between the driver and the void in the dashboard, where the radio should have been. Only then did Naji Awad understand that the strange voices were echoing nowhere but inside his own head.

When the taxi arrived at its destination, it pulled up next to a gas station. Naji Awad got out and walked through the alleys of the town, making his way toward the unlicensed clinic owned by an unlucky doctor who had never finished his medical studies. He had opened his clinic twenty years earlier and, since that time, had been performing abortions, mending the hymens of sinful girls, and treating patients wanted by the police, all while taking advantage of this dark street and its few passers-by.

Naji Awad stood next to the door of the clinic and stole a look inside. He saw the doctor sitting in the lobby under a dim light. Next to him were three companions smoking shisha and watching a wrestling match on TV. It's true, he had broken into this clinic on more than one occasion to blackmail its owner and make deals with him, but he was sure the man wouldn't recognise him in his new state. However, he would certainly recognise his voice. He lowered his head and began to think for a few moments. Then he made his way toward it, hunched over, feigning pain in his side.

Behind a cloud of opium smoke, the obese doctor looked at him intently. He tossed the remote to the side and got up, gesturing for Naji Awad to move toward one of the doors, where he gave him a shot of a strong pain reliever. Naji Awad's head spun for several seconds before his limbs froze.

Regaining his wits, he asked the doctor—his tongue twisted and tied—to treat the wounds on his skin. The doctor didn't say a thing. He examined his face and neck and lifted his shirt. When he saw the flayed skin, he asked in a clinical tone:

– What's the cause?

– Gas.

– Gas?

Before he could even say a word, Naji Awad tossed a stack of cash in his face. The doctor snatched it and put it into his pocket, then said:

– Take off your clothes.

Naji Awad undressed completely. The doctor was shocked when he saw the peeling skin. He pointed to a nearby chair. When Naji Awad sat, the doctor attached an IV bag and began cleaning the burns on his skin with iodine and covering them in silver sulphate cream.

Suddenly, one of the doctor's companions made his way toward one of the cupboards. He scattered its contents and took something from it. He turned around and stared for several moments at the body of Naji Awad covered in ointment. He took a deep breath and said, pointing with a wobbly finger:

– I don't know where I've seen this man.

Immediately, Naji Awad's senses activated. He moved his eyes quickly toward the pile of his clothes, where his gun was concealed. He raised his eyes toward the speaker, who continued, now more sure of himself:

– Yes, I've seen you. I don't know where though.

Naji Awad was positive that this man would discover his identity in the next few seconds. His face contracted, and he began to reach for his gun on the floor to shut that loudmouth up. Seconds before he could do that, the doctor turned to the man, swore at him, and shooed him away. He then came back and got down to business. A moment later, he straightened up. His eyes locked on Naji Awad's, and he calmly said:

– There was no reason for you, Mr. Officer, to come here. It would have been better had you called me, and I would have come to wherever you wanted.

Naji Awad didn't respond, but kept staring at him vacantly. When the doctor started to say something, he curtly interrupted:

– Finish your job or else I'll rip your heart out right now!

The doctor went back to his work, frightened and confused. He didn't dare say another word. When he had begun to clean between the man's thighs, he saw his tiny member. Due to his experience, he understood what that meant. He became even more confused. Naji Awad noticed his hands shaking. He asked for a cigarette. The doctor quickly got one from a drawer in his desk. He lit it with two trembling hands. Naji Awad exhaled a puff of smoke then ordered him to close the door.

When the doctor had finished his work, he covered Naji Awad's skin with a layer of gauze infused with codeine. He then removed the IV from his arm and gave him a shot of penicillin and let him get dressed again.

Naji Awad felt a vitality course through his veins. He stood in front of a wide mirror while he fixed his clothes. Pointing to his face, he asked the doctor:

– And what about this blackness?

– It will go away. It will disappear as the skin renews itself.

Naji Awad walked toward the doctor's desk and sat behind it. He began to play around with his things for a few moments then grabbed a cigarette pack and lit one, saying:

– I don't want anyone to know I was here.

The doctor answered while washing his hands in a filthy sink in a corner of the room:

– Of course, of course. No one will know.

Naji Awad took a pair of surgical scissors from the desk drawer and surreptitiously slipped them up the sleeve of his shirt. He then got up and walked toward the doctor, who was drying his hands next to the sink. When he turned around, he was startled to see Naji Awad standing behind him—staring at him with lifeless dark eyes, not a spark in them at all. The doctor took an involuntary step back and, before he could say anything, Naji Awad pulled out the scissors with a quick motion and planted them up to the hilt in the doctor's chest. Enraged, he said:

– Sorry. I don't trust anyone. Ever.

The doctor let out a stifled gasp, and his pupils dilated from pain and fear. His hand grabbed the handle of the scissors that had impaled his chest, and he took two steps forward. He leaned on his desk for a few seconds, then fell to the floor, blood spurting from his mouth and nose. After his body had gone entirely limp, Naji Awad dragged him, piled him underneath his desk, and then walked out of the clinic, the lobby long since vacated by the night owls.

He didn't forget to lock the clinic door behind him. He crossed over two streets then hopped in a taxi, taking it to a neighbouring town. There, he rented a room in a dilapidated hotel after showing an employee the doctor's ID card, which he had stolen from his desk drawer. In his rundown room, he undressed with great difficulty. In the dark, he sat next to the window, tossing down a drink from a small bottle, wrestling against the meow of a cat that echoed inside his head. Suddenly, the sound went away, and he was able to get a hold of himself. He was thinking about Fathiya and that phone call. He tried to explain it away, but he couldn't. All the evidence indicated treason and nothing more.

He heard soft raps on his room door. At first, he thought it was an aural hallucination, just like the sounds that bounced around his head. He kept ignoring the knocks and, after a few minutes, he glanced at the door and saw a shadow move beneath it. He got up slowly. He grabbed his gun and hid it behind his back. He opened the door a crack. A boy carrying dinner looked back at him. He reached out and took the tray, then closed the door. He turned on the bedside lamp and lifted the cover over the tray. Inside, he found cold bread, fried *fasouliya*, and slices of red onion. Sitting on the edge of the bed, he began to eat pieces of *fasouliya* with his fingers. Just then, he remembered his personal computer and how a few days earlier he had copied the contents of his wife's phone on to it. He wiped his hands on the bedsheets and set the tray out of the way. His senses were on high alert. He put a lot of the blame on himself: Why hadn't he looked at the phone contents out of curiosity? Now, and in light of the new data, the phone's contents would be the decisive proof. It wasn't just incontrovertible evidence, but it would give him peace of mind and justify any future action he might take.

Chapter 13

Ziad Al-Niqash

January 5

The third day

I opened the gate to our courtyard and, at the very same moment, the door of our house opened as well. From within the darkness, my mother appeared. She looked sick. When she saw me, she wasn't shocked, nor did she smile, but instead she reached her trembling hands toward me. The whole affair was strange, and I had never seen her this way before. The girls were behind her, holding back their tears. I shouted: Where is my father? Hinaa responded by pointing toward the grapevine. Strangely, he was standing beneath it, staring mournfully off into the distance. Before I could make my way toward him, a large black dog with a clipped tail and ears jumped between him and me. He bared his teeth at my mother, and she and my sisters recoiled, closing the door behind them. The dog turned around, taking a step back, and then lunged toward me. I jumped and let out a loud terrified scream.

Frightened, I opened my eyes only to find myself stretched out on a roof. The sun was on the cusp of rising as I caught my breath and lowered my hand, thinking about the dream that had come over me. Everything in it revealed that something evil was lying in wait for my family. Oh God, remove this evil and its fiends!

I got up, performed ablutions, and then prayed *fajr*. Anxiety continued to roil within me. I tried to call my mother, but to no avail. I turned off the phone and put it back in my pocket. When the sun began to cast its first rays, I left the farm. I looked all around for a moment before walked purposefully southward, toward what seemed to be the end of this verdant valley.

I stopped next to a lush date tree. I tied my shoes and, before I could stand up straight, heard the last sound a person would want to hear in such a situation: a rifle being loaded. Yes, with absolute clarity, I heard a weapon being loaded. I heard the sound of metal coming into contact with a bullet as it left its cartridge and entered the firing chamber. Something heavy in my throat crashed down and settled violently into the pit of my stomach. My throat went dry, and my bladder filled up completely. I didn't dare turn around. I raised my hands high and announced my surrender. I tried to say something, but there were no words or even letters in my mind.

I trembled violently, stammering out a few words that were drained of all life by fear. Meaningless nonsense twisted out of my mouth. I felt the muzzle of the rifle plant itself roughly against the small of my back. A sharp aggressive voice said:

– On the ground! On the ground!

I knelt and said, with fear in my voice:

– I'm unarmed! I'm not carrying a weapon.

Someone else came over in a hurry and asked:

– Who is this?

He jabbed me with the muzzle of his rifle:

– A soldier. I found him here.

He poked me again and asked:

– Where did you come from?

Before I could answer, the man who had just come up said:

– It looks like he survived the ambush yesterday.

Quickly, he made his way toward me, slapped the back of my head, and said with disgust:

– Damn your father, you son of a bitch!

– Terrified, I said:

– I...I...I'm...a conscript. I'm not a soldier.

One of them responded:

– What's the difference? All of you are fucking bitches.

He struck my neck with the butt of his rifle and then yelled:

– On the ground! On the ground!

I lay down on the ground, trembling and tried to explain myself, but my words shrivelled up, dissolving into rapid panting, crusted over with dirt from the ground. One of them stepped on my neck. I felt incapacitated, as if the end was near. I clung to the ground as tightly as I could, hugging it. Yes, I lost my strength and hugged the ground. I hugged it to the point of absurdity. I appeared as if I were trying to disappear between its arms, ribs, and chest. A cry escaped from me, and I lost control of my bladder. Other footsteps arrived on the scene. I cast my gaze through the mud and branches toward the horizon. I gathered what I could of my strength and screamed in a voice filled with tears:

– You're wrong! I want to speak with you. Just listen!

Two bare feet caked in mud up to the calves stopped next to my face. The foot that had been stepping on my neck was lifted. Before I could take a gasp, the owner of the two mud-splattered feet kicked me violently in the face so that my body flew sideways. I opened my eyes and let out a deep moan while cradling my bleeding mouth.

I found myself prostrate on the ground in front of three staring men who stood before a backdrop of date palm leaves. A rifle, axe, and scythe dangled from their alert hands. The one with mud-covered feet took large strides as he came toward me. He kicked me again in the flank and I screamed out in pain. My body doubled over. Perhaps my scream whetted the men's appetite to kick me more. A swirl of kicks rained down on me, and my hands and arms failed to soften the blows. Blood ran from my mouth and nose, and I surrendered to the pain. It was as if I found myself tumbling down a deep, dark well where all sound transformed into a distant rustle.

Before I could close my eyes, I saw a rope in one of their hands as the man came to wrap it around my neck, and then forcefully jerked me onto my back. The rope pressed so hard against my throat that it tore my skin. He pulled the rope up harder, forcing me into a standing position. Blood and saliva erupted from my mouth, and I was on the verge of death. I shoved my fingers between the rope and my neck, but his hand was stronger and even more merciless. He slackened the rope causing me to fall onto my back, then wrapped it around my hand and pulled me once again through the mud and thorns. My back slammed against the trunk of a huge date palm. He yanked the rope up, making me stand, then pulled it violently once more. He tied my neck to the trunk while standing on my right, his hand gripping the rope, his face near mine. I turned to look at him from behind the veil of blood and pain. He wasn't the devil I had imagined, just a violent peasant with a round angry face that had been pockmarked with acne long ago. When he realised I was looking at him, he pulled the rope tightly and said contemptuously:

– You want to see me? Memorize my face because it's the last thing you're going to see in this life.

Blood and my very soul gurgled in my throat. He continued:

– Have a taste of your own medicine.

He stopped speaking then violently plunged his fist into my face. One of the two men came forward and punched my stomach with the butt of his rifle. My body bent backward, letting me take in a deep breath as it did. The man holding the rope didn't give me any more room, but bared his teeth and forcefully yanked the rope back toward the tree. My body slammed back, and my head collided with the trunk as my backbone cracked and my rib cage contorted. I coughed and threw up blood and saliva.

Blows, kicks, and head butts rained down on me from all sides. They beat me with everything they had. From behind the haze of blood and pain, I saw their faces take pleasure in what they were doing as they vented their anger. Their faces betrayed an unquenchable thirst for revenge, after they'd been taken by surprise with an opportunity to exact it. I realised there was no escaping their grasp. No remnants of compassion would make a path to their hearts even if my body were ripped in shreds. My eyes filled with hot tears that went flying with each blow. Lumps gathered in my throat while a cloud of pain took away my breath. Sapped to the depths of my being, I began to fall into an abyss of unconsciousness.

Guys, I'm not the Messiah who should atone for the sins of mankind. I did nothing to deserve this punishment and don't deserve to die. I'm just a pawn that left the battle before I'd even entered it and before I even knew where to find the battlefield. O, cruel stroke of pain, be done! O, prayers of my mother, I need you now! O, ashamed tears of my father, intercede on my behalf! O God! All good deeds that you have done in this life, save me now from these executioners. You in your heavens, who knows how I've been wronged, spare me from this grinding torture.

Blood poured from my mouth, nose, and ears. Blackness began to swirl across their faces and their voices transformed into an irritating ringing. One of them twisted a metal chain around his fist then slapped my face. My head ricocheted violently against the tree trunk. Moaning, I coughed out a spray of blood that covered their faces, the fields, and the distant mountains. One man pulled the rope tighter, pinning me further against the trunk while another grabbed me by the neck and said with disgust:

– Shhhhh!

I held my breath. The men looked toward the sky with concern. They froze. A far-off boom made its way to our ears. As his eyes swept the horizon, one of them asked:

– A jet?

The other responded to him, placing his hand over his head, his eyes scanning the sky:

– K..k...katyusha!

Before he could finish his sentence, a sharp whistle pierced the sky from the east and dive bombed out of range. A terrifying explosion echoed, shaking the date tree and everything around us. Another whistle followed, and then a loud boom. Then explosion after explosion. Everything happened so quickly it was as if the sky were raining down fire and flames and volcanoes were erupting. Columns of smoke and dust rose toward the sky. Penned animals became agitated and birds fled their nests. Dogs howled plaintively in the fields and deserts. One of the men got up, running and shouting in a panic:

– The houses! They're shelling the houses!

One followed after the other. The man holding the rope around my neck loosened it for a few moments. His eyes scanned the area. When he realised what he needed to do, he wrapped my neck forcefully with the rope then drove me toward a one-room side building with an iron gate in front. He wrapped the rope around his hand but found it difficult to take the keys out of his pants pocket. He glanced toward the dust and columns of smoke that were rising skyward, becoming more confused and agitated. He yanked the rope down as he burst into tears and said in a voice filled with heavy panting:

– Get on the ground here you son of a bitch!

He stopped talking and grabbed a scythe that was dangling from the trunk of a neighbouring peach tree. I laid down on the ground. He stepped on my head then put the scythe under his armpit and pulled out the keys from his pants. He began to thumb through the clutch of keys in a disorganized manner. Filled with tears and terror, his eyes travelled between the keys and my body and the horizon billowing with smoke and dust. No doubt he was in the worst possible state of mind—just as I was in the worst state mentally, physically, and emotionally. With what little consciousness I had left, I realised that he wouldn't hesitate to sink that scythe into my body if I didn't cooperate. I heard him crying. He kicked the door violently. The door opened with a jarring clang. The man wiped his eyes and nose with his shirt sleeve and, in a shaky voice, he said:

– Inside, you son-of-a...

I crept toward the inside. Closing the door firmly, he then ran off shouting as loud as he could:

– O Lord! O Lord!

Before his voice had petered out, there was another sharp whistle. I lay on the ground, protecting my head with my arms. A powerful explosion boomed, shaking the area. Things from the roof and walls fluttered down and the air filled with dust before everything went quiet.

I sat up, straining to listen. Suddenly, all the pain in the world descended upon my body. I stretched my leg across the ground. Pain overwhelmed me. I couldn't stop myself from crying. I cried with my entire being. By the time my tears dried and my reserves of whimpers ran out, my body had become adjusted to the pain and mocked it with a false serenity. I took off my shirt and began to dry my wounds and wipe off my blood. I spat blood over and over. Resting my back against the wall, I closed my eyes as I tried to distract my mind from everything that had happened and began to think about what I was facing.

Of course, it didn't end there. Perhaps God's sympathetic hand postponed my assault until an unknown time when it would continue, as it had begun and perhaps would even worsen. I didn't know if I would survive the next time or not. I would be an idiot if I thought that they would treat me properly after the shelling had targeted their homes. Staying here meant that I was dead. No question about it. I had to get out of here as quickly as possible.

The room was cold, damp, and dark except for a few rays of light that filtered through an opening under the door and cast off some of the darkness. The place was crammed full of farming equipment. I stood up, stumbling about in pain and headed to the door. With no luck, I tried to remove it. I went to the back and pulled out Suleiman's lighter from my pocket and flicked it on. I began to look for a tool that could get me out of there. I took down a hoe from the pile of farm equipment. I tried it against the door, but the door just clanged. I lowered my head and began to think. I examined the walls and found that they were built with mud mixed with straw. I set the lighter with its flame on a barrel beside me. Before I could begin digging into the wall, an exhalation came from one of the corners.

At first, I couldn't believe my ears, but the sound repeated, followed by a feeble cough. I tightened my grip on the handle of the hoe. I took the lighter and made my way toward the source. I raised the lighter, trying to dispel the darkness in the corner. As the shadows fled, I saw a ghost of a person heaped into the corner.

I shouted nervously:

– Who's there?

The response was low and filled with groans and coughs. I gathered my courage and carefully crossed through the chaos, toward the source of the voice. The stench of blood and cold sweat slapped across my face. The veil of darkness that had obscured the face of this body fell away. I was shocked! Terrified, I jumped back. It was the son of the Vietnamese woman! I placed the lighter on the ground and moved toward him. I asked:

– How did you get here? What happened to you?

He responded feebly:

– I'm dying. I'm dying.

I looked at him closely. I found him cold and limp. Blood soaked his clothes and the ground beneath him. He pointed to his abdomen. Unbuttoning his shirt, I saw holes next to his navel. Blackened blood oozed. I took off my shirt—or what was left of it—and tore it into pieces so I could make bandages for his wounds. I held his hand. I wasn't in the best state, but I told him encouragingly:

– Be strong! We will get out of here before they come back!

He could only reply with a suppressed groan as he feebly squeezed my hand. I grabbed the hoe and lighter and went back to digging in the wall. A violent explosion echoed, shaking the walls. The room's interior heaved with dust. I stopped digging. An idea came to me—I could moisten the walls to make digging easier. I set the hoe off to one side. I undid my belt and emptied my bladder against the wall. I resumed digging, squeezing out all the strength that remained in my body.

I realised full well that I had only one option and that was to escape, and I had only one safe chance to make it happen. I had to take advantage of it completely. Outside, choices and possibilities were numerous. But between these walls, choices were nearly non-existent, and seeking help other than through flight was impossible.

After the sixth or seventh strike, a part of the wall collapsed. I moved toward the opening. I spit a mixture of blood, saliva, and dirt and worked quickly to widen the gap. Setting the hoe aside, I grabbed my lighter and went over to where the son of the Vietnamese woman was laying. I lifted him by his armpits, and we headed out. We walked through the valley, in no specific direction. He was weak and fading. He could barely move his feet or raise his head. Still, we kept moving. Sounds from this way and that trailed us while the echo of feet running along the bends of the pass came out of nowhere. Illusory eyes watched us from behind the trunks of trees. We didn't stop.

Suddenly, the roar of a jet plane in the sky above the valley reached us. It completed two circles in the sky then dropped its missile. We heard it tear through the sky, and then a violent explosion sounded. I looked back. Beyond the intertwining trees and branches, I saw columns of smoke and dust rising along the not-so-distant horizon. I knew full well that the army would not let yesterday's attack go without response. But what was the villagers' crime to warrant this shelling? And even if some of them had a hand in what happened, that doesn't mean their houses should be flattened over their heads or that their dismembered body parts should be ground into the dirt!

After hours of crossing through fields and farms, my strength was drained as we arrived at a dry valley with barren hills and no vegetation at all, except for a few thistles. I glanced around aimlessly at the desolation of that wilderness. We set out southward. The sun's flames were above us, and below our feet was a hellscape of pebbles and thorns. After about three hundred metres, the son of the Vietnamese woman collapsed. Limp, he fell to the ground. I shook and slapped him. He feebly opened his narrow eyes and tried to say something, but his chapped lips smothered each letter.

Helpless, I looked around. I couldn't leave him there, nor could I wait for him to regain his strength and continue walking! I had one choice. I put him on my back and began walking. I heard him rave and ramble incoherently. He wept. I tried to talk to him, but he paid no attention. He just continued his hallucinations and wailing.

Sweat stung my wounds. Weakness overtook me from within. My steps became heavy, and my body began to stumble. I heard a sharp sound above. I stopped and, while panting, raised my eyes to the sky. A vulture circled us. I lowered the son of the Vietnamese woman and rested him against a nearby rock. I sat beside him to catch my breath. His moaning was soft and low now. I tried to comfort him by telling him white lies. I told him everything. Except the truth. There was nothing more I could do for him than what I had done. Despite all that, not even the smallest trace of a response appeared on his face. He just kept moaning in his delirious state and his face became extremely pale.

I stood up and looked all around. I felt that I was standing in place, as if I were walking in a vicious circle. Landmarks and the entire area all resembled each other. But I had to keep moving. Time was not a luxury I had. I took off my shirt and dried the wounds on my face. After I had finished, I wrapped my head with it and resumed walking, carrying the son of the Vietnamese woman on my back. After several minutes, I heard him speaking incoherently in Vietnamese. When we reached the edges of a clearing, he said with a heavy tongue:

– You are so good, you son of a viper.

Adding to what he had said, he muttered a few words in Vietnamese and went silent for several seconds. Then he let out a long laugh that stopped me in my tracks. I began to say something, but he let out a long gasp before his head dangled back awkwardly, almost toppling me over. I lowered him and placed him on the ground. I shook him and slapped his cheeks, but he had gone cold. Silent. Pale. No trace of life remained in him at all.

I stood up, scared. My eyes looked around the wilderness that had become even more desolate. The wind howled, carving sullen faces and gaping mouths into the calcite rocks that had been barren since time immemorial. I don't know how long I spent next to the body of the son of the Vietnamese woman, staring at him in shock, completely powerless. I didn't know what to do when I heard the sound of the vulture. At that moment, I thought of Cain and Abel and the crow.

I got up and dug a grave with whatever I could find among the dried branches and sharp rocks. Then I pulled the corpse to the bottom of its resting place and covered his face with some grass. I shovelled dirt onto it and finished the grave by building a triangle of rocks above it. Since I didn't know his name, I wrote on the grave marker with a piece of limestone rock: "Son of the Vietnamese Woman, 5 January 2018."

I left the grave behind me. The vulture accompanied me as I walked, directionless. I was hounded by the desolation and faces and voices of those who had died. I became resigned to the fact I would never escape this. It was impossible that death would offer me an escape. Everything here told me that.

My strength slackened. Dizziness encompassed me. And dryness choked my throat. I knelt, raising my eyes to the burnished sky. I saw the vulture still hovering high above. The faces of my mother and father never appeared.

This was the end. No doubt about it. There was nothing else but this. Alright, let's just end this torture. I decided to let my body tumble to the ground. Before I could fall, I looked off at the far horizon. My senses awoke. I regained my balance. I stared deeply at a point on a distant plateau. I couldn't believe it. I tried to forget all the swelling around my eyes and peered even more intently at that spot. I realised that I wasn't looking at a mirage. It was a tri-coloured flag fluttering on top of a communications tower at the summit of the plateau!

It was an army position!

I got up. I struggled to drag my feet. Finally, an unexpected ending to all the fatigue and fear that I had experienced was in sight. Feebly and weakly, I ran. I arrived at the bottom of the plateau and stood next to a huge cactus plant, waving my shirt toward the bunker. My mouth was parched, but I called out, yelling over and over. No response. Everything became distressing before my eyes. I wasted no time and decided to climb up. A few steps up, and dust and pebbles scattered down on my face and chest. A sharp whizzing sound crossed my head, and another grazed my arm. Before I realised what was happening, the valley hills and plateaus echoed with the sound of gunfire. Then there rushed out a stream of blazing bullets on the dirt, rocks, and plateau. They were getting closer, hitting the ground, boring holes into it, and tossing up burning shrapnel into the air!

A cold wind blew. I heard my father cry out my name in grief, the door of our house creaking and then slamming shut. I heard my sisters muttering and the horn of a strange car crossing the empty street. I realised the last chapter of the story had arrived, taking me by surprise. I closed my eyes in surrender. My fingers let go of the shirt. I welcomed the next shot with a limp body, an empty mind, and half-raised hands. I heard my mother crying in fear.

Suddenly, two strong hands plucked me from my place and dropped me behind a large boulder. I saw glowing bullets burrow into the ground where I had been standing, scattering dirt and sparks into the air. The bullets stopped. I shouted out in a loud voice. I called to them, and they answered with a barrage of fire, which splintered the cactus bushes and tossed dirt and sparks up in my face. I left my spot and moved, protecting myself with the boulders. Suddenly, I found myself in front of the barrel of a rifle being pointed by an armed, dishevelled man wearing military pants and a cartridge on his bare chest. I raised my arms and said, terrified:

– E....e....easy! Take it easy!

His worn-out face contracted. Then, in an explosive tone, he said

– Who are you?! What are you doing here?

– I...I...I'm a conscript. I was on the truck and...

He extended his hand and cut me off:

– Your ID card. Show me your ID.

I slid my hand into my pants pocket, bewildered. I pulled out a bundle wrapped in a plastic bag and held together with a rubber band. He took the bundle from my hand and began turning it over without opening it. He saw my mobile stuffed in between the papers. He shook his hand, saying:

– You have a mobile?

I nodded. He threw the bundle toward me and said:

– Are you armed?

– No.

He approached me carefully and gave me a quick inspection. Out of patience, he said:

– Where do you think you're going?

– I...I...I don't know. I'm looking for somewhere safe and a way back to my home.

He stared at me several moments then raised his rifle and rested it against his shoulder. He said:

– Stay here. Don't move.

He went away quickly, taking shelter behind the boulders. My eyes followed him until he disappeared behind one of the rocks. I sat on the ground, weak and feeble. Minutes later, he returned. Cracking his knuckles, he said:

– Okay, get up and walk in front of me!

We ascended a rocky corridor, then stopped at a sharp bend blocked by a large boulder. Next to it was a small slot big enough for one person to pass through. He called out in a hoarse voice:

– Abu Nizar!

We heard a muttering coming from behind the boulder and out popped two men wearing army fatigues, looking weak and dishevelled. One of them wore a Real Madrid jersey and the other had on filthy underwear. The two of them were in a deplorable state, revealing that months had passed without them washing or cutting their hair. They looked me over for several moments. The one in the filthy underwear put his rifle on his shoulder. My escort said to him:

– This is him!

Abu Nizar nodded, then stuck out his lips and said:

– Well, we don't have any space here for him. Even if we had space, we don't have any food to offer him.

His words shocked me. Fearfully, I said:

– But where should I go? I don't know the way!

The other one asked me:

– Where's your weapon?

I looked around at their faces. I began to respond, but Abu Nizar beat me to it and said:

– Figure it out yourself. We have orders to not receive anyone.

I looked over at my escort, who kept staring at the two of them, his face not revealing anything. I said:

– How do I manage it myself? I'm your comrade! How can you leave me in the open country?

Abu Nizar spat between his feet for no reason. Then he lowered his rifle and let it hang down. His wagged his left index finger in my face and said, angrily:

– Figure it out yourself! We have enough problems as it is. I advise you to get far away.

He stopped talking and turned to leave. As for the other one, he kept staring at us with his finger on the trigger. My escort held my arm and pulled me to the side. He said:

– Wait here.

He disappeared behind the boulder for a few moments. I heard voices rise and lower. The last voice I heard was my escort saying sharply:

– Good!

My escort came back and stared at me for a few seconds. Then, rubbing his unkempt beard, he said:

– Okay, let's go. You'll stay with us for a little while.

I walked with him several metres beyond the boulder, then found myself at the top of the plateau, inside the military position. The fort was spacious, with bunkers spread throughout—some demolished and others rebuilt with sandbags, sand blinds, and old tires. Holes and wreckage were everywhere. Even the iron communications tower was riddled with holes from bullets and rockets. Explosions had caused parts of it to collapse.

In this spacious area, there were only maybe twenty scrawny soldiers led by Abu Nizar. They made me enter one of the bunkers and the soldiers brought over a medic, whose visage appeared to me like the face of the Messiah. He treated my wounds and gave me an IV, then went away and came back with an old military shirt stained with blood that had been dried for months and some simple food and water.

After a little while, Abu Nizar showed up. He welcomed me and apologized for the soldiers who had fired on me before he went away. I learned from the medic that the military fortification was in a constant state of high alert in preparation for armed attacks that nearly never stopped. A day didn't pass without one of them falling. The medic informed me about everything then began to silently stare into my eyes. I felt that he wanted to ask me about what had brought me here, but he pulled back and instead removed the IV from my arm and left me alone.

I sat up and put on the shirt as I lowered my head to think. I struggled to grasp the situation. The soldier I had first met below the plateau came over to the bunker. He repeated what I had heard from the medic and added that they were suffering a shortage of soldiers and expecting an attack at any moment. For no reason, I kept looking at his withered face. I found myself submitting to his command. He smiled. Then he came closer and patted me on the shoulder before he went away and returned, accompanied by another soldier named Bahloul. He informed the man that I was a conscript and ordered him to give me an appropriate weapon and ensure that I knew how to use it. Bahloul moved his head without saying a word. He then gestured for me to follow him toward one of the fortified ramparts where there were several machine guns of various calibres. Bahloul eyed them intently for a few moments, then came up and took a midsize machine gun and gave it to me, saying:

– The BKC is right for you. It works great and only needs a little cleaning.

I muttered something in reply, and he added:

– I'll clean it and teach you how to use it.

Bahloul disassembled the machine gun quickly and cleaned the parts with oil before he put it back together. He loaded it with ammo and took one shot into the air. When he finished, he gave it to me, and I carried it over to a bunker that had been shot up with bullets and placed it against the sandbag wall. He taught me how to fire and load it then gave me four grenades and patted me on the shoulder, encouragingly, and went away.

It seemed that there was no escape from this war or from this torture! Every time one part of it ended, I found myself in front of yet another! It seems that there is no end in sight. Oh, Ibn Al-Niqash, you really have fallen. You don't even know where you've fallen from. It would have been safer for you to have kept walking along your route undercover. You might have even made it to safety. And if you didn't, then you would have at least benefited from a comfortable death, which is not what currently awaits you.

Bahloul came back and gave me an old helmet, a bottle of water, and a sack of dates. I asked him

– Where do you expect the attack to come from?

– They will come from all directions. Mostly, they attack with over-whelming fire and manpower. We have to reciprocate just to stop them.

– How?

– Aim your machine gun toward them and squeeze the trigger. Never lower your head and don't let them advance one step! You have to cover a semicircle with your shooting, from right to left. Your comrade will take care of the other half.

He finished talking then left. With my eyes, I traced the semicircle he had indicated. A few metres away, there was a burnt-out BMP tank next to grave markers of those who had died here. Abu Nizar appeared suddenly, asking me to give up my spot for another soldier and to station myself in another area to the right of the camp. I carried my weapon and settled in. Again, I sketched out a semicircle. A few metres away from my new barricade was Bahloul's position. Within moments, I realised he was an expert RPG thrower. He waved at me from his bulwark, where he stood between three wooden crates and had three loaded rockets in front of him. He took off his shirt and shoes. He rolled up his pantlegs to below his knees, then put on his helmet and placed a big stick of gum in his mouth. With the energy of a true expert, he lifted the rocket onto his shoulder, saying:

– Like that. That's better and lighter.

– Are they coming?

– Yes, I'm sure of it. When we saw you below the plateau, we thought you were one of them.

– That's why you shot at me?

– Yeah.

– ...

– Yesterday, one of the rocket launchers was destroyed. Look over there; it's next to the tank.

– The launcher was destroyed?!

– Yeah, from the godawful amount of shooting. Its metal heated up and melted. Don't worry about all that. Focus on your semicircle and fire your weapon like hell and don't let a single fly pass. Especially when I stop to reload the launcher. Our work has to be in sync.

I nodded. Then I began to examine the magazine of bullets and added two more sandbags to the screen. Suddenly, a strong explosion echoed in one of the bunkers, spraying rocks in every direction throughout the fortification before it was followed by successive explosions in various areas. Bahloul shouted:

– Mortar! Get on the ground!

I huddled down deep in the rampart and watched balls of fire and columns of black smoke, followed by rockets. Bahloul shouted out from the bottom of his bunker:

– That's just the beginning with mortar shells. They'll attack once it's over. Be ready!

No sooner had he stopped talking than a barrage of bullets roared and rained over our heads, striking everything in its path. Bahloul called out:

– Now! Let's go!

He got up and fired his first rocket. I raised my machine gun and squeezed the trigger, shooting at everything in my semicircle: boulders, dirt, trees, the ground. I didn't want to kill anyone, just prevent them from advancing. I didn't want the war to stain me with its filth even if it led to my death. Bahloul kept launching rockets one after the other. The air filled with dust and the scent of gunpowder. I reloaded my weapon and went back to shooting. Bahloul was firing his rockets and shouting ecstatically, as if the situation for him was a kind of pleasure, a daily routine. He called out while adjusting his helmet:

– There, over there next to the water tank!

I turned my weapon. I saw armed men running toward one of the bunkers. I shot a round between their feet and they retreated. Bahloul shouted:

– Good, good. Next time raise your weapon a little and aim at their chests.

I began to say something, but a violent explosion echoed between me and Bahloul. The explosion ripped me from my barricade and dropped me far away, onto the gravel and thorns. I tried to get up and move but couldn't. Explosions kept coming. Flames licked my face. From behind the cloud of smoke and dust, I saw armed men storming our position and firing in every direction. Before I could close my eyes, I saw Bahloul crawling on the ground and then a big red bubble of blood exploded.

Chapter 14

The Family of Muhi Al-Deen Al-Niqash

January 6

The fourth day

When the sun had risen, the light revealed the extent of the catastrophe. The shelling left behind a wide gash six feet deep where the tent had once stood. It was filled with black water and floating on its surface were shreds of burnt clothing, single shoes, bottles, and lumps of roasted flesh. All the houses that overlooked the tent, including the mayor's home, had been destroyed by fire and no longer had windows or doors. Anyone looking at them would think they were faces with the eyes plucked out.

Several elderly men had volunteered to help and were carrying plastic buckets. They pushed through the line of gawkers with their feeble bodies and henna-dyed beards and heads and, despite their weakened eyesight, began searching patiently in the walls and crevices for scattered human body parts, their lips trembling, their muttered words not understood.

Cars arrived from the neighbouring towns carrying bolts of white fabric. The bundles were distributed among the women whose eyes burned with tears. They carried them on their shoulders and walked toward the school that had been opened.

At nine in the morning, the men transported the corpses from the courtyard of the clinic to the town mosque. The men's bodies were laid out in rows in the mosque's courtyard while the women's were moved to the garage of one of the wealthy people in town, so that the women could dress and appropriately prepare them. The air filled with the stench of blood, grilled flesh, and burnt clothing. The men began to ready the bodies in the courtyard but did so slowly due to the lack of volunteers. When help from the neighbouring towns arrived, they were allowed to prepare the bodies on the tile of the grand mosque courtyard once sheet curtains had been set up, borrowed from the surrounding houses.

In the largest room of the school, the air was warm and hung with sadness. Heavy-set women in their fifties sat at the pupils' desks, their eyes puffy from weeping, and began to cut the fabric into equal-sized squares to wrap the bodies. Despondent young girls gathered up the pieces and placed inside each one a bottle of perfume, a tablet of camphor, and a bundle of rosemary. They then folded and put them into a large basket.

On one of the tables, my father set six shrouds that he had bought and whose fabric had been dipped in the water of Zamzam years ago. When the war broke out, my mother began to prepare them for each member in our family. My father looked around at the faces and began to say something, but the words shrivelled up inside him. He bent his head and lifted his sleeve to wipe the tears that started to fall from his eyes. He turned and went out toward the barren hill where the men of the town, and those who had come from other villages, had gathered.

There, on that desolate hill, the police chief, who was in full uniform, informed them that a delegation from the capital was coming to participate in the burial of the victims. He confirmed that satellite TV stations would also come to cover the event. Some thought the idea was good while the majority were upset. When those who were upset tried to discuss the matter, the chief told them that he planned to convince the authorities to regard the victims of the accidental shelling as martyrs and approve a monthly stipend for their loved ones, just as they did for true martyrs. That guaranteed to shut everyone up.

About an hour and a half later, the police chief's phone rang, and he picked it up and went off by himself. When he had finished the call, he came back over to the men whose faces were pale and moustaches coarse and informed them that the authorities apologized for being unable to come due to security considerations, nor would any representatives from media outlets be able to attend.

The men muttered among themselves, then disbanded and regathered below the giant oak tree. At length, they discussed the number of graves and their shape, finally agreeing to dig one grave for all the victims. They took their spades and shovels and lined up next to each other and began earnestly and in unison to dig up the soil. After hours of backbreaking digging, a hole appeared in the barren ground, as if it were the mouth of a mythical monster gaping toward the sky. In an instant, thunder clapped and a cold drizzle poured from the sky, tamping down the dust and easing the exhaustion of the workers who stood in the hole.

Suddenly, a hum off in the distance reached them. Everyone looked toward its source and, after a few moments, the buzzing distilled into the sound of "Allahu akbar" and "There is no God but God," and everybody saw the first of the coffins being carried on shoulders, trailed by a stream of people.

All of them made their way toward the large gravesite. The coffins, cloaked in green fabric, were set one by one on the edge until there were fifty-three. Despondency draped their faces and weeping stifled their words. The mosque's imam recited the funeral prayer and all present lined up shoulder to shoulder in a singular act of intimacy. The grieving appeared as if they were embracing one another to lighten the weight of the sadness that was crushing them all. At the cemetery gate, women and children gathered in throngs, the sound of their crying rising and falling as if being scattered haphazardly by the drizzle.

After the men had finished the funeral prayer, some of them jumped into the hole while others began to lower the coffins with ropes, one after the other. After the last one had been lowered in, the men made way for the women and children to take one last look. Crying rang out and dirt scattered on everyone's heads. Children sobbed. The situation pierced all in attendance and nobody was able to hold back their tears.

As the rain began to pour, the men took their spades and shovels and filled in the grave with an intensity equal to their sorrow. The sound of gravel and dirt falling on the wooden coffins rose into the air. And as the coffins disappeared under the earth, the women realised there was no escape from accepting the truth of the final departure of those who had passed. Half an hour later, everything came to an end. Nothing remained of those resting in the coffins other than the upturned black topsoil and the memories held by the newly widowed women and weeping throngs of children beneath the trees.

My father and mother returned home. Neither the downpour nor the mud stopped them on their way back. As they approached the house, my mother shivered involuntarily. At that moment, a white tuft of hair that had never been there before fell from her temple. My father sat on the ground, his chest echoing the sound of his quickened breathing. Without changing her clothes, my mother drank her coffee while my father sipped a cup of mint and zaatar before going to bed. The pain and sadness were more than any could bear.

The thunder clapped and my mother pointed toward the phone, her hand limp and lethargic. One of the sisters passed it to her, announcing that there was a message on the screen. A half smile worked its way across my mother's face as she read the text. She muttered with deep gratitude:

– So, he is well! Praise be to you, Lord.

The cold night descended mournfully and suffocatingly. Nobody in the town closed an eye while the smell of gunpowder and death continued to linger in every corner. A cold January-evening wind howled, carrying with it waves of faint groans that filled hearts with fright.

The evening's first news bulletin didn't mention the event. People waited for additional news, but their wait was in vain. At eight in the evening, the news announced that the country was in the path of an oncoming storm from the high seas, and that it was carrying volcanic ash. That was the lead story on all the channels.

Meanwhile, two groups of stray dogs gathered on the outskirts of town along with eighteen wolves that had come from the distant flatlands. The dogs knelt on the ground and let out a continuous doleful howl, bordering on a cry. As for the wolves, they ascended the barren hill and began to bay. It was a frightening and plaintive yowling that no one had ever heard before.

There were those who firmly believed that the end of the world was nigh. And there were those who said that catastrophes are what make the wheel of history and demography turn. As for the vast majority, they had lit all their lamps and retreated into the corners in terror, eagerly awaiting the dawn, so they could leave town and never return.

My mother talked to Ragheb for quite a while after she had tried to contact me with no luck. While talking with him, she winkingly asked him for the hand of his daughter, Rajaa, as a bride for me. Uncle Ragheb was silent for a few moments, then his laugh rang out throughout our nervous home. Without hesitation, he announced his agreement. My mother's face lit up, and she told him that the wedding would take place during my first leave when I returned home.

He didn't disagree at all, but welcomed it. She finished the call and spoke to the girls, smiling. Then without any prior thought, she took the phone and dialled my number. She wanted to give me the good news. My phone rang, and her face brightened. She told the girls that the phone was ringing, unlike the last several days. Delighted, they gathered around. The ringing ended with no response. She tried again, two more times, and then a third. It was no use. She attempted to hide her anxiety with a wan smile, then said:

– Perhaps he's away from his phone. We'll leave a message. I am sure that he'll see it and won't waste a moment in calling us back.

Summoning all her eloquence and affection, she wrote: "My darling son, only a few days have passed since you left us. We feel as if it has been years. How are you and where are you now? We are all doing well and send you our love. Today, I arranged your engagement to Rajaa, your uncle Ragheb's daughter. She is an upstanding girl, and we will not find anyone better for you. I agreed with your uncle that the wedding will take place during your first leave, when you come back home. Be well, my son. Be well."

She set the phone down and then went to her room. She wanted to tell my father. When she opened the door to the room, she was shocked to see him lying face-down in the middle of the room. She froze in place for a few moments, unable to scream or do anything. She rushed toward him and turned him over; blood was issuing from his nose and mouth. For the first time in her life, she let out a painful scream that filled the whole universe. At that very moment, the sky in our town rained down cold, volcanic ash, filling the air with the stench of sulphur.

Chapter 15

Naji Awad

January 6

The fourth day

Naji Awad opened his eyes to the sound of the imam finishing his early morning prayers at the large mosque opposite the hotel. He kept staring at the ceiling without understanding or absorbing where he was. Then suddenly his mind recollected all of yesterday's events, awakening his senses at once, and he sat straight up in bed.

A violent swirl of pain struck him, and he felt his tight skin tear with the slightest movement. He suppressed his reaction to the pain and stubbornly got up. Grabbing his flask, he took a swig. His stomach contracted, and he knelt and emptied his insides onto the floor. Panting, he got up and slowly got dressed. He didn't know how he would make it through his day in such a state. He sat on the side of the bed and took a loaf of stale bread, gnawing on it while taking a gulp from the flask. When his stomach was full, the alcohol did away with most of his pains, and he finished putting on his clothes and slid his gun under his shirt. He stood in front of the mirror, taking a hard look at his face, which had become unsightly, more bloated and blacker than it had been the day before. He raised what remained of his eyebrows and, before he could let out a sigh, he heard the voice of Leila Mourad singing: "My heart is my guide...my guide...my guide..."

He looked back at the ceiling, toward the window and beyond, remembering the sounds of yesterday. He left the room, paid the hotel manager, and retrieved the doctor's ID card. As he left the hotel, the voice of Leila Mourad still echoed inside his head.

As he got in a taxi headed toward his town, her voice disappeared. After a quarter of an hour of peace, the sound of radio static boomed once again in his head. Spontaneously, he grabbed his ears and almost screamed in pain. He took two sedatives and tried in vain to ignore the sound, to occupy himself with observing the road. The road to the village was bumper-to-bumper with long lines of vehicles carrying aid and volunteers to the town. The car stopped, not moving an inch. The pain returned. He took as big a swig from his flask as he could muster. Time moved slowly, and he felt irritated. He paid the driver the fare and got out of the car and bounded past the traffic and cars. In the distance, he saw a temporary military checkpoint blocking the road. He thought about turning back. He didn't want to risk it. Before he did, he saw groups of people bypassing the blockade on foot. He didn't waste any time and joined them, then got in the first taxi and high-tailed it out of there.

The town's streets were empty. Its air was filled with the smell of gunpowder and charred flesh. At that moment, the sky rained down a cold drizzle. Camouflaging himself against walls and in alleys, he kept walking. He tried to ignore the voice calling after him insistently. When he arrived at his house, he entered through the back door after checking to make sure nobody had seen him.

He listened closely and, when he didn't hear the slightest sound, he went into the kitchen and took a knife, slipping it into the sleeve of his shirt. Then he headed toward the bedroom. Slowly, he opened the door. Something huge collapsed inside of him when he saw the bed was empty. His nose filled with mucus. The remnants of hope coaxed him out of his frozen state and forced him to investigate the remaining wings of the house. When he didn't find a trace of his wife, he scolded himself, the whole world, and the devotion he had affected for so long. He spat in the face of the universe and took off the guise of the devoted husband and put on the garb of the dirty officer. He opened his closet and took out his personal computer, then opened the safe. He was shocked when he didn't find any of his wife's money or her clothes, while his money was still there, not a cent missing. He emptied the safe and put its contents into a handbag. Then he locked it back up.

He sat on his bed and flipped on the computer. Up until that moment, he had still been hoping and wishing. As he opened the copied files, he thumbed through the contact book. Nothing caught his attention, except that it contained only five numbers. He wrote them down on a piece of paper and began to navigate through the messages. He found one hundred-twenty texts. Eighteen were from the service provider and one-hundred-and-two were sent from a "Nadaa Jaber." He clicked on the first of the messages and muttered:

– Let's see what we have here.

It was a normal text message, about an appointment on Thursday at eleven in the morning. The second text also contained an appointment. The third held a long number, as if it were a bank transfer. He began to close the file, but before he did, he decided to open one of the old texts. He chose one at the bottom of the list. He was horrified when he found it was a flirtatious text. He opened all the messages, one right after the other. Most of them were chatty texts, nothing amorous, between the sender and receiver.

He lowered his head for a few moments, then clicked on the sent messages folder. He opened the first and the picture came into focus. The sent texts corresponded to the received ones. He jotted down the number of "Nadaa Jaber's" phone and the number of the phone itself. He went back to flipping through the contents of the file. He didn't find anything important. He grabbed a bottle and a bar of imported chocolate from the small refrigerator by his bed. Taking a bite and a long sip, and muttered:

– Let's get back to work!

He opened Google and typed Nadaa Jaber's phone number into the search bar. He clicked *enter* confidently and, after a few seconds, several results popped up on the computer screen. He chose "Mobile Service Subscriber Numbers."

He clicked the link and a blue page opened before him, sporting the logo of the main mobile company in the country. He clicked the contact list for subscribers and entered Nadaa Jaber's phone number in the search bar, then waited for the result. After a few seconds, the result popped up. The number was registered in the name of "Nadeem Jaber." He raised his eyebrows and muttered:

– A simple difference

He took a swig from the bottle and placed it off to the side. Thunder pealed outside and raindrops began pitter-pattering against the windowpane. He entered the number of the phone that had received the messages into the search bar. After a few moments, a result appeared: Fathiya Attallah. He shook his head sullenly, pressed a key on his computer, and muttered:

– Let's see who this Nadeem Jaber is!

He went back to Google and typed Nadeem Jaber into the search field. Google took him to Facebook. He clicked on the link to the sole result, and it brought him to Nadeem Jaber's page. He waited a few moments before he was facing the picture of a man in his fifties—time had eaten away at him and drinking had left him emaciated, with sunken eyes and jaundiced skin. He read through his posts and found the last one was from March 2015. He muttered:

– It's not him. I'm sure of it.

He searched for the name on Facebook, but there were no other results. He had barely connected when, at the last moment, the connection dropped. He lowered his head and began to think. Outside, the voice of the muezzin at the large mosque wafted over to him, announcing that the prayer for the victims would be in the cemetery.

His eyes roamed over to the white curtains and suddenly the persistent voice started calling him again. He looked right, then left, pretending to ignore it. The voice went away for several minutes before it returned, this time with a chorus of voices, all overlapping. His headache returned, too, and he took three sedatives, all while muttering profane curses. He sighed as he batted away the dozens of mouths encircling his head.

He closed his eyes and tried to focus on the task before him. It occurred to him to search for the phone number within Facebook itself. He entered the number in the Facebook search field and hit enter. After a few moments, a webpage bearing the name "Majnun al-Hawa" appeared on the screen. He smiled victoriously when the picture of a young man in his thirties looked back at him. He knew from the man's profile that he was a music teacher and managed a music institute in the capital. He copied the picture onto the computer. He studied it carefully and imprinted everything in his memory. After he was satisfied, he read through all his posts, but didn't find anything that piqued his interest. Most of them were ads for dance classes, while others were for piano lessons. He wrote down the name of the institute and its address. Then he turned off the computer. He kept staring into space, his face not revealing any impression one way or the other. He put the computer back in the closet and reorganized the area, then left the house as he had entered it.

Rain began to pour, reawakening his pains. But he had to keep going. He left the town and hopped in a taxi to the train station. From there, he got on the first train headed to the capital. He sat next to the window, lost in thought as his face clouded over. Something strange was telling him that she was in the capital, now that she had realised he was dead. He wished the wheels of the train would cross the distance in the blink of an eye. His heart was burning, and his pride was haemorrhaging. It would not be enough to rip out her heart and crush it under his foot, not her heart alone, but the heart of that musician as well.

He would not be forgiving this time. A person can give up one of their limbs, but is it possible to forsake someone altogether? In a certain way, she had done just that. He should have realised it from the very first hours of her silence toward him, but he had been overcome by wishful thinking. Yet there was still time, and surely he would rip her out of his life and uproot her from his soul. He would do all that in his own way, satisfying his thirst for revenge and filling his soul with comfort and calm.

The train stopped at a station along the track. Some passengers got off and others got on, along with some policemen and itinerant vendors. He kept his gaze on a distant flame burning away from atop a metal tower in an oil extraction field. The policemen passed next to him, scrutinizing everyone's faces. A feeling of danger grew inside him. He saw a newspaper on the seat opposite him and took it, burying his face in it. Suddenly, one of the policemen stopped beside him and blew a whistle. The other officers in the other cars all rushed toward him. The blood in his veins froze. He did not lift his head from behind the newspaper. The policemen swooped down on a man sitting nearby. The man tried to resist and jump from the window, but a policeman wrapped him in his arms and the other cops rained down blows with their clubs, then led him away, handcuffed and drowning in his blood. Meanwhile, Naji Awad didn't budge an inch and continued to feign sleep.

After a few moments, the train started to move again. Three hours later, he arrived at the capital. He made his way toward the first cafe he happened upon at the train station. By that time, he had transformed into a disfigured monstrosity whose body was oozing pus and emanating a sulfuric stench. Eyes judged him harshly, but he didn't care. He filled his stomach then bought a hat, pack of cigarettes, and two small bottles of alcohol, along with some pain relievers.

Donning his cap, he walked among the crowds. He stopped next to a light pole and took a gulp before putting the bottle back in his pocket. He lit a cigarette and walked over to the taxi stand and got in. He handed the driver a small slip of paper with an address written on it. The driver read it quickly, then gave it back to him with the tips of his fingers while looking intently at his face for the eighth time as the car took off down the streets of the capital. Thirty minutes later, it stopped in front of a modern five-storey building and the driver pointed toward it, saying:

– That's the address.

Naji Awad paid the fare and got out. He stopped and stared at the building and at the numerous placards hanging on its facade. He felt dizzy. He regained control of himself and quickly walked toward it, holding firmly to the strap of his handbag. He asked the doorman which floor the Pietro Crispi music institute was on. The doorman told him—with a look of sheer disgust—that the institute was on the third floor. He began to enter, but stepped back and asked the doorman:

– Is Mr. Nadeem Jaber here today?

The doorman nodded. Despite his pain and the presence of an elevator, he chose to go up the stairs. When he reached the third floor, he found it was a large open room walled off by translucent glass. Inside, a piano rang out with a dance melody. He stopped, retreated to a corner, and caught his breath before he carefully withdrew his revolver. He pulled out a cartridge clip and placed it into his pants pocket, his finger on the trigger. The music stopped and rapid and boisterous clapping broke out.

Three young girls exited the large room, laughing as they passed by. They didn't take any note of his presence. He caught the scent of a perfume heavily accented with notes of orange blossom. Something strange stirred in of him. Encouraged by the devils inside him, he took a step forward and stopped beside the door. The piano began playing a new melody, more delicate and playful than the one before. He poked his head through the open door and saw pairs of male and female dancers gliding along on the shiny floor of the dance hall. The air was filled with laughter and liveliness. Suddenly, he saw what he had come for: a young man in his mid-thirties with long hair and a full face. It was Nadeem Jaber— only slightly different from the picture on Facebook. He was dancing with one of them and smiling. Static ricocheted inside his head for several seconds, then he heard a hissing sound whisper:

– That's him right in front of you. Go on, take revenge. Put an end to your pain. Take revenge for the sake of your dignity. She tore out your heart, so now tear out hers! It's not a difficult thing. Go on! Go on!

He looked side to side, then pulled out his revolver. Suddenly, Nadeem Jaber turned around in a dance move, giving him his back. He started to raise his gun, but his heart broke and instantly his strength went limp when he saw the face of the man's dance partner. It was none other than his wife, Fathiya. His wounds were inflamed by burning sweat. And though his hand trembled, he whispered, egging himself on:

– Not bad. Two targets with one shot! What an advantage fate has offered you. Even events are on your side. Go on, finish what you came for. Then take your money and flee this country for some place where nobody knows anything about you and start your life over, so you can enjoy calm and peace of mind for the rest of your days.

He batted away an illusion that hovered over his head and tried to raise his gun again, but a thousand hands snatched his hand, and another thousand hands tore out his insides, emptying his veins of the blood, pus, and sweat that were inside his body, leaving him hollowed out as if he had been created of flimsy paper. Dizziness overcame him, and he made an effort to stay strong. When he failed, he propped his body against the glass wall. He saw her standing on his feet as he moved her about here and there, resting her head on his shoulder as he did. He whispered something to her, and she raised her head and gazed into his smiling face.

Her face was beautiful and bright, pulsing with life. She appeared more delicate and beautiful as he kept staring at her while volcanoes and seas wrestled within him. Suddenly, out of the blue, he lost all his strength and the devils in his mind flew off in an instant. He took an involuntary step back. The playing stopped. Applause and laughter rose. In this moment of retreat, he heard her laugh, but it wasn't that jeering laughter that had made him go crazy in the distant past, nor was it the scandalous laughter that he'd always hated. It was something beautiful that he had never heard before.

He left the institute defeated, unsuccessful, and weakened. He walked aimlessly and unconsciously in the streets of the capital, over its bridges and through its markets. He neither heard nor saw anything. He took a detour down a side street. The world shook him violently as scenes passed before his eyes. He stumbled then knelt next to a trash dumpster and emptied his stomach. At that very moment, the wounds in his body began to spurt a yellow, sulphur-scented liquid. He rested his back against the dumpster and pulled out his bottle, emptying it in one gulp then tossing it away. He kept staring mindlessly at passing figures. A light wind blew, tossing up a fistful of dirt onto his body. Someone chucked a sack of trash from a speeding car and it collided with the dumpster, sending its contents flying all over him. It didn't faze him at all. After thirty minutes, he appeared to passers-by as a homeless person. The voice inside his head whispered mockingly:

– What's happened to you? What's all this weakness? What's with all this dejection? You are the executioner of the Ministry of the Interior! Are you not the son of evil and the blood shedder? Are you not the untamed son? There now stands a divide between the myth you once were and what you've become. Pain and torment have a way of cutting haughtiness and arrogance down to size, but they don't destroy everything. When the influencer ceases to exist, so too does the material change it has wrought, just as a passing wind eventually dies away. Have you ever heard of an eternally blowing wind?

He was no longer able to open his eyes or resist the numbness. Scenes began to fade away and voices grew more distant. He smiled a smile devoid of meaning. From behind the curtain of his exhaustion, he saw two legs standing in front of him and a mongoloid face approach, then he saw an additional pair of legs and heard the amplified echoes of a nearby conversation. He felt a brush of cold wind and the taste of dirt in his mouth. He didn't care. The person with the mongoloid face reached out a hand and pulled the bag out from between his legs. He tried to open his eyes and grasp at his clothes, but in reality he could only feebly move the tips of his fingers. He heard a loud crack. The hand of the young man reached out and scattered everything in Naji Awad's shirt pocket before they both ran off, leaving him behind. He wanted to scream, get up, and chase after the two thieves, but his inflamed body, crusted over with wounds, collapsed into the trash, bathing in the ammonia and putrid decay.

Chapter 16

Ziad Al-Niqash

January 6

The fourth day

The chill of dawn stung. I opened my eyes. I kept looking at the ceiling, replaying in my mind all that had happened. A terrible ache throbbed in my right ankle and jawbone. At one point, I noticed the stench of something rotten that filled the place. I sat upright and found myself in a windowless room, its walls blank and coated in dirt. The scent of gunpowder seeped from my clothes. At some point, I recalled opening my eyes and finding myself tossed into the back of a pickup truck beside a corpse wearing a military uniform, the stench of blood and dust filling my belly. When was that? I don't know. I'm not sure if I truly had seen it, or if it was all a feverish dream.

The sun sent its first rays through an opening in the roof, revealing the ugliness and filth around me. It looked like a hastily built livestock hovel where empty crates and old shoes had been discarded. On one of the walls, there hung poorly tanned animal pelts that reeked with the stench of worms and decay. Large blue flies had burrowed deep into the hides. In vain, I tried to get up but fell back down.

So now what? Where was fate taking me? And how much more could I bear? I had no idea when my walls would collapse and my last fortress of inner strength would give out. I thought this was the end. Could I even ask how it would all end, trapped as I was between the hands of these people?

The matter didn't require a lot of smarts. The ending was predestined. Its inevitability was not up for discussion. Everything else was nothing more than trivial wishes and utter nonsense.

The pile of shoes caught my attention. I crawled toward it. There were many more than I expected and in various sizes. I pulled out a single white shoe and found a splotch of blood on it that had dried months before. I tossed it onto the pile, then went back to my spot scared and confused. Suddenly, a scream came from outside. The scream of a terrified man, in pain, pleading for help. Punctuating his cry was some muttering and the sound of a car engine leaving the area, along with the voice of the frightened man.

Suddenly, the door opened and two people entered. One was wearing a cartridge bag and a rifle dangled from his hand. The other one was thin, short, and bald, he and carried a stack of papers in one hand. The short one stopped in the middle of the room. I got up from where I was sitting and leaned against the wall, standing on my good foot. He swept his gaze across the ground and saw a cockroach quickly cross toward him. He crushed it with a foot more than was necessary. Then, raising his eyes toward me, he calmly said:

– Hey, what do we have here?

Another armed man approached and placed a chair in the middle of the room. The interrogator sat down, placed one leg over the other, and crossed his hands in his lap. He leaned back and gestured for me to take a seat, which I did with great pain. He gave a dry smile, through which I could see his sparkling teeth and blackened gums. He said calmly:

– Where did they bring you from?

Through the pain, I stammered out an answer:

– Uh...uh...

Every letter that exited my mouth gave rise to a volcano of pain in my head. Blood and saliva trickled between my swollen lips. I pointed toward my jawbone. He lifted his thin hands from his lap and wiped his bald head, then put them back beneath his armpits. He kept staring at me, then pursed his lips and said in a low voice:

– You can't talk? Alright!

He took a pen from his pocket and disassembled the sharp pieces, removing the ink tube. He placed the pieces in his shirt pocket and set the ink tube on the stack of papers and gave them to the armed man. He gestured at me with his head and said:

– But you can write, correct?

I nodded, yes, then took the papers and pen from the hand of the man with the gun who was still standing beside me.

The interrogator continued:

– Write down everything about yourself. Everything. And when you finish, knock on the door.

I nodded. He got up immediately from his chair and turned around to leave. Then he stopped and looked back toward me, saying:

– Do I have to tell you what happens here to liars and deceivers?

Before I could get out a trace of an answer, the armed man standing next to me stepped on my injured foot and crushed it under his rough boot. My scream of pain echoed and reverberated off the walls of my cell, bouncing toward the sky. The armed man lifted his foot. The investigator smiled, then left. The armed man spat on the wall and stepped back while staring at me. He took the chair and left.

When I regained my composure, I gripped the pen and began to write without stopping. I wrote everything as it had occurred from the beginning until the moment the armed man had stepped on my foot. I don't know how long I spent hunched over the papers. When I finished, I got up and leaned against the wall. I walked slowly toward the door. I knocked and it opened. Before I could say anything, a dusky hand reached in, and I gave back the papers and pen and then returned to where I was sitting, listening to my aches and to the explosion of images and sounds that began to erupt inside me.

I remained in confinement without water, food, or visitors. I heard the sounds of cars, some coming and others leaving. The sounds of fighter jets circling in the sky above. The screams of people, as if they were being torn apart limb by limb. And sporadic gunfire. It was as if I were in hell. Hell couldn't be anything other than this.

When night fell, I continued waiting in the darkness, fighting off armies of insects and mosquitoes. Suddenly, the door opened, and an armed man approached carrying a gas lamp. He hung it on one of the walls and left. Then he came back with a chair. After several seconds, the bald interrogator came in. I stood up. He placed the chair in the middle of the room and sat down. The interrogator, placing one leg over the other, gestured at me to sit. He remained silent for a few moments, then raised his eyebrows and said:

– You look to be in good health!

I wasn't, but I nodded and with difficulty said:

– Pr..praise be to God. I...I'm okay.

He smiled drily then said:

– Good. You can speak now.

I nodded. He opened the stack of papers then licked his thumb and began flipping through them slowly, one page after another. He stopped on one and perused it for a few seconds. After he finished, he tapped on it with a finger and, without lifting his gaze, said:

– You said you were in the Istiqbal encampment...

I interrupted him:

– In the rear guard of the Istiqbal camp. I learned later that that place wasn't the Istiqbal camp, but was the rear guard, located somewhere else.

Slowly, he raised his eyes toward me. The armed man rushed up to me and swooped down onto my injured foot, crushing it with this hard boot. I screamed out in enough pain to fill all creation. Then he left me writhing in pain. The interrogator didn't pay much attention, but remained silent, watching what was happening. He let out a long exhalation before he stroked the tip of his nose and said:

– You said you were at the Istiqbal camp. Were you trained to shoot and carry a weapon?

My eyes shot between the face of the interrogator and the foot of the armed man, and I said in pain:

– Yes, they trained us to shoot.

He shook his head, licked his thumb, and began to thumb through the pages. He stopped at one and asked me:

– Where were the trucks taking you?

I answered him, my eyes furtively glancing at the foot of the armed man.

– They didn't tell us.

He let out a small, sarcastic laugh and turned the pages once more. He stopped on one and said:

– You said a man saved you from the army's firing. Why did he do that?

– I don't know!

– How many soldiers were at that position?

This time, I glanced at the interrogator's face, the armed man, and the open door. I answered:

– I don't know exactly. Maybe twenty soldiers.

He exhaled again and said:

– So, what do you know! Are there other survivors besides yourself?

Wiping away the burning sweat that covered my face and neck, I answered:

– I didn't see anyone other than the son of the Vietnamese woman, but he was gravely injured. He couldn't hold on and died. I buried him in the valley. Everything is written there for you.

– And who were the soldiers?

– I don't know!

He went silent for a few moments and stared at me, indifferently, before he gave a jaundiced smile.

– Now, tell me in detail about what went on in that military position.

I began to narrate the events that had taken place as they had occurred and as I had written them in the papers that were in his hands. However, he threatened me, unconvinced of the truthfulness of my statements and searching for something that wasn't there at all. The armed guard stepped on my foot twice more and I felt the bones in my feet crumble. The interrogator seethed with anger. With a menacing shout, he stood up, drew his gun, and pointed it at me. Suddenly, three armed men approached. When he saw them, the interrogator's lips dried up and he nervously wiped his bald head. One of them rushed up, saying:

– How is it going?

He answered the man tensely:

– He insists on what he said. He has given me nothing new. We think...

The armed man cut him off with a wave of his hand and directed a question at me:

– Are you hiding anything that you want to clear up?

I shook my head and asked him:

– Like what?

He gave a horrible smile before he said:

– A GPS locator chip that can lead planes to where you are...communications equipment...anything of the sort?

I shook my head again and confirmed:

– I am carrying nothing. All my possessions are with you. My phone and everything else.

His face dried up and contracted. His eyes moved toward the armed man who was crushing my foot as if it were his profession. He barked at the man:

– Strip search him.

The armed man was confused and moved toward me, followed by the guard who had just entered

– Inspect under his fingernails, even if you have to pull them out. And under his eyelids if necessary, even if you have to rip them off.

I stood up and leaned against the wall. They ordered me to strip off my clothes, all of them! Then they inspected my body cell by cell. They searched my clothes, piece by piece and fold by fold, and then threw them back in my face. I grabbed what I could and covered up my lower half.

The armed guard who had come in last muttered something, then said:

– Search the room carefully!

He finished talking, turned around, and went out. The armed man rifled through the room inch by inch, and on his face was a look of irritation and annoyance. When he had finished his search, he stood there panting and shook his head. The interrogator said to me, as if making a vow:

– If you're hiding anything, we'll definitely find it. and you'll wish that you had never been born!

I leaned forward to pick up my clothes from off the ground and asked, while pushing past my pain:

– And if I'm innocent?

He pressed the tip of his finger against his lips then moved it, saying:

– The judge will decide!

The interrogator stopped talking and shoved the stack of papers under his arm and turned around to leave as the armed man trailed behind him, carrying the lamp in one hand and the chair in his other. Then he slammed the door behind him shut.

I could hardly put my clothes back on. I rested against one of the walls and listened to my aches. I don't know when sleep finally overtook me, but when it did, I dreamed I saw the camphor tree in our courtyard shaking, its branches falling and collapsing, demolishing the western corner of our house. I saw myself and my mother and sisters gathered around it. We were crying. My father wasn't there. My mother knelt beside the tree and began to slap her face and chest in lamentation, scattering her hair in the wind as the sky rained down a blackness that covered the whole scene.

I woke up startled, confused, and scared. It had been a strange, incoherent dream, but unravelling its mystery was not difficult. I realised—and I truly hoped I was wrong—that my father had left us. Not only us, but our world.

I didn't sleep the rest of the night. I was surrounded by a vision of my father, and his scent welled inside me. I heard his mutterings and remembered everything he had said to me. Every shout he shouted, both to scold and to advise me. I remembered him working diligently in his workshop, plaster dust covering his beard. I remembered his delicate fingers sculpting the plaster, handling it, and turning the pages of his Quran. I remembered him grave-faced and upset under his grapevine, chewing clove seeds. I remembered...I remembered... My whole soul was filled with his scent. My sobbing stifled my breath. I cried as if my heart were aflame, as if I were in more agony than anyone on earth.

I tried to convince myself that it was just a muddled dream or that I had misinterpreted it—but, in truth, I had I felt something profound was taken from my chest, leaving behind a huge hole, with nothing but the wind howling through it.

Chapter 17

The Family of Muhi Al-Deen Al-Niqash

January 7

The fifth day

A morning dawned, strange and despondent, the likes of which the town had never before seen. The sky was ashen and bleak as volcanic cinder rained down and covered everything, filling the air with the stench of sulphur.

My mother devoted the hours of the night to preparing and washing my father, then she carried him to his bed, covering his body with a green blanket. She closed the door and sat beside him, staring at him in silence. True, in the first minutes, she had been surprised by his passing. But she quickly pulled herself together and gathered the weeping girls around her. She told them that they had to be strong and to do the necessary to the fullest, in a manner that would make their father happy. The sisters accepted what my mother said, dried their tears, and got to work as if nothing had happened, much to the astonishment of the neighbours.

After my father had been laid to rest, my mother stood beside his grave, my sisters behind her clad in black, offering prayers to God and reciting verses from the Quran. Afterward, they planted five jasmine shoots, each with the name of a family member on it. My mother chose the shoot with my name and placed it exactly in the middle of the gravesite, then all departed the cemetery.

Meanwhile, the town groaned under the weight of grief and pain. Nobody knew where they should go to offer condolences, since sorrow had visited every house and tears were in every eye. A collective feeling of despair and helplessness seized those who remained. Others left everything behind, carrying what they could of their possessions, and left the town for good. The village vanished under twenty centimetres of ash, which continued to fall, and people stopped using the water from the well after it started to taste of sulphur. The ash killed agriculture, flowers, and scorched the leaves of trees. Everything was marching toward the precipice, or so fact after fact implied.

At the doorstep of our house, my mother and sisters dusted off the ash from their clothes and stepped inside. At that time, it was cold and dreary, although the air was filled with the scent of perfumed plants and rosemary. As they prepared for the mourning ceremony, my mother and sisters appeared more composed than all the women from the town who had begun to come in throngs.

Amidst the muttering and mumbling, my mother's phone rang. My mother reached for it and raised it to her eyes. When she saw my name floating on the screen, her face clouded over, and the phone nearly fell out of her hand. She got ahold of herself and kept staring at the screen, asking herself: Why is he calling now? I wonder if he knows something happened? Who told him? Someone from the town must have called or at least sent him a text, but if he doesn't know...I don't want him to know!

The phone went silent. My mother looked around at the mournful faces, then set the phone on a small table. It rang again. She took it and turned off the ringer and placed it back on the table. After two minutes, the phone rang another time. One of the ladies called out:

– Is everything alright, Umm Ziad? Is there something wrong?

My mother glanced between the wrinkled lady speaking and the phone screen, then said nervously:

– It's Ziad calling. I don't want him to know what has happened.

A thin elderly lady broke down into tears and said:

– His heart must have felt something!

The phone went silent. Another lady shouted:

– Answer it and put his mind at ease! Tell him anything. If you can't, give me the phone and I'll answer it.

My mother shook her head and said in a voice that was trying to be strong:

– If he calls back, I'll answer. I'll see what I can say to him.

Eyes locked on the phone in my mother's trembling hand. Deep within her heart, she was hoping the phone would not ring again. She wished this with the same ferocity that she had wished the opposite ever since I had left. One of my sisters lowered the volume on the Quranic recitation that was playing. Silence filled the space for several minutes until it was broken by whispering. Then the phone rang. My mother stared at the screen for several seconds. Suddenly, something frightening swelled within her, and her left eyelid twitched while her pupils dilated and her face darkened. With a shaky, hesitating finger she pressed the button, then the speakerphone, and began quickly speaking:

– Hello? Ziad?

Static and garbled noises came through. She shouted again, but the call ended. She kept looking at the phone in dismay. Her breath returned, echoing in the sitting room and drowning out every sound. An immense terror wriggled into her soul. Her limbs quivered. She didn't wait for the call. She redialled the number and waited several seconds. The line opened. She cried out:

– Hello? Ziad? Ziad?

The voice came through loud and clear, reverberating in the sitting area, but it wasn't my voice. The voice's owner said:

– Are you Umm Ziad or his sister

She cried out in grief:

– I'm his mother! Is he okay?

The women's necks craned, and their faces clouded over. The voice responded:

– He's fine. He's with us now.

Muttering rose. She got up and stood, then cried out in a panic:

– With you? Who are you? Where is Ziad?

The man with the skull tattoo on the back of his hand responded:

– We are the Revolutionary Liberation Movement. Your son, Ziad the soldier, is fine. He was taken captive on the battlefield and he's fine.

She cut him off, weeping:

– He's not a soldier. Let me speak with him!

The speaker went silent for several moments, during which she could hear his breaths and a voice shouting in the distance. Then he said:

– That's not possible now. He's not here with me.

She cried out, imploring him:

– I beg of you. Let me hear his voice!

He responded to her after a moment of silence that betrayed some hesitation:

– Please. I can't. All I can tell you...

He was quiet for a moment. It seemed as though he were fighting back a lump. In a hoarse voice, he continued:

– All I can tell you is that he has been convicted and...

Tears flowed from my mother's eyes, and her heart beat erratically. She cried out:

– Huh? What? He's my only one! His father passed away hours ago. The soil on the grave is still wet. We have nothing left in this world except him. Shame on you!

The speaker remained silent. She heard a gurgle in his throat and the sound of a tank rolling by. The women began to murmur and cast glances at each other. The voice sounded hoarse on the speakerphone. As though he were lowering a heavy weight from his shoulders, he said:

– The court condemned him to death, and the verdict will be carried out within hours.

My mother screamed.

The women screamed.

Bodies boiled over.

Chapter 18

Naji Awad

January 7

The fifth day

Naji Awad opened his eyes to a sharp sound, the rubbing of rusted metal joints. He found himself tied to a wooden chair in the middle of an entry-way lit by a flickering blue neon light. He saw wet blood on his bare feet, which were stretched out before him on the tile floor like two intersecting lines pointed toward the closed door. His eyes roamed around the cold room and gazed at the solid massive walls, where humidity had begun to eat away at the paint. Again, he heard metal on metal. His body got goose-bumps and he smiled wanly. Swallowing saliva that tasted of pus, he fixed his eyes on the door.

The voice inside his head whispered mockingly:

You've fallen, you son-of-an-emaciated-woman, you've fallen into a den of wolves and you will never leave, except torn into pieces and scattered among 365 plastic sacks. That should make the feral dogs in the alleys of the capital happy. Or perhaps fire will devour the bags in one of those bio-waste incinerators. It appears the situation is horrific, eh? And why not? Didn't you yourself spend a period of your life in a room like this? Working outside the law, flaying skin, inflating abdomens with airguns? You know full well what goes on in these rooms and that there is no room for compassion or mercy. Look over there. Don't the streaks of dried blood on the grouting in the tile floor remind you of something? And what about these elongated black splotches on the walls—have you seen them before? Do you know what they are and how they are formed? I don't think you would forget something like that.

Enough with this shit! Tell me what brought you to the capital, eh? You should have taken your money and left this country any way you could! What insanity drove you to punish your wife's lover? Hahaha. Does that phrase bother you? He's her *lover*. What do you want me to call him? Her friend? Her teacher? A man who has more manhood than you? Ha. Uff, look how our conversation has been derailed. Let's get back to the crux of the issue and the truth that you try to ignore and deny. What is that truth? Fathiya impaled you. The Impaler came at you from an unexpected direction. Haha. So there is nothing you can do besides accept all the consequences. True, it's an emotional, "soft" impalement with no physical trace, and it won't make you fear for your ass or guts, but it will rip out your heart and shred it to pieces, my friend. Haha.

The sound of footsteps on tile echoed, then stopped. Three masked men wearing civilian clothes entered the room. Sweat had left stains under their armpits and on their chests. It was the executioner and his minions. A large key ring unused by anyone dangled from one of their belts. He shouted, lewdly:

– Get ready, you son of an emaciated woman!

He gazed at the intruders with a vacant expression. The masked faces meant that their work was extrajudicial. He knew this from his time working in the room back in the day. He saw one of them carrying a drill. One of the masked men approached and outlined a circle over his heart with a cotton ball soaked in iodine. He stopped for several moments, during which he seemed to be thinking about something. Then he approached, exposed his leg, and drew circles over each knee.

He cried out in panic:

— Are you going to kill me?

No one answered. Fed up, the man who was holding the drill said:

— What's with the other circles? Let's pierce his head and be done with it. I don't have the energy to clean up the room.

The one carrying the keys said:

— You were supposed to spread out the tarp under the chair. A traitor like this doesn't deserve clemency or the benefit of a quick death. We need to rip him apart and scatter chunks of him in the city's trash dumps.

Backing up two steps, the one holding the cotton ball added:

— Okay, let's get this over with.

Naji Awad tried to slip out of his zipties. He tried to scream, but to no avail. Everything was prepared so it could be done calmly and quickly. The one holding the drill came up to him. He felt the man's breath on him. The one with the cotton balls approached, muttering something under his breath. He drew a circle on his left temple and another above his eyes and another on his throat. He stopped suddenly. He seemed to be thinking, then he randomly slathered Naji Awad's face with spots of iodine. The one holding the drill pushed him aside and placed the tip of the drill over his head. The buzz of the drill rang out inside his head. A volcano of panic erupted inside of him. He tried to break the bands. He tried to scream.

Terrified, he jolted upright.

He stepped back and collided with the wall. He gasped loudly. His eyes darted fearfully around him. He found himself still next to the dumpster, in front of a hairless, malnourished dog that was licking at Naji Awad's wounds and face. He threw an empty box at the dog, and it scampered off, scared. He pulled his thoughts together. He heard the sirens of police cars as he leaned against the dumpster and feebly got up. Pus and blood oozed from his body worse than before. He pushed down the pain and walked along the walls toward the train station. Eyes looked at him in disgust, provoking him. He was exhausted beyond belief. He stopped to rest. The thieves hadn't left him with anything except his gun on his hip and a 50-franc note in his pants pocket.

He walked toward a small cafe that served fast food and juice and heard a television blaring the news bulletin. He moved closer until he was near the flatscreen TV hung by the entrance. His picture flashed continuously on the screen. A photo of him in his military uniform, his picture in civilian clothing, a recent picture he didn't remember taking. The anchor began to narrate his crimes. Then he announced a reward of 10 million francs for anyone who came forward with information about his whereabouts.

All his senses were on high alert. He took a step back, his eyes watching faces preoccupied with their food and whispers. Suddenly, a firm hand landed on his shoulder. He looked back, petrified. The face of a young waiter who had been following the television from afar took him by surprise. He pushed him outside roughly and informed him that he was unwelcome in the cafe. He smiled ruefully down in the depths of his soul. He wanted to say that the man had shoved away 10 million francs with his own two hands. However, he was content with a sad smile. He pulled out some money and handed it to the waiter. Before he could say anything, an olive-skinned teenager nicked the money and disappeared into the crush of bodies. The waiter pouted his lips and shook his head, then gestured for him to leave.

Dragging his heavy feet and utterly discombobulated, Naji Awad left. As he arrived at the train station, his pain and dejection reached their climax. At that moment, his chest cracked and his shoes filled with blood and pus.

He stood on the platform. Black blood poured from his nose. He wiped it away with the sleeve of his shirt.

The voice in his head roared with laughter, then whispered mockingly and gloatingly:

– The journey has ended, bitch. Acknowledge your losses, you gambler. You soldier. You sure know how to rack up losses! Didn't you once say that when a horse's strength gives out and old age gnaws away at him, it's killed with a mercy shot out of compassion and respect for the animal?

Naji Awad nodded into the wind and then said, with a dry mouth:

– Yes, I said that. Yes, I said it.

The voice continued in the same tone.

– But you never were a thoroughbred horse, were you? You were a rabid dog. And rabid dogs are killed out of respect for the ones they harm.

The taste of pus and blood welled up in his mouth. With trembling hands, he pulled out his wallet. He glanced at his military ID and an old picture of Fathiya. He started to smile but didn't. He closed the wallet and tossed it into the gutter. He looked up toward the dark sky. A cold wind began to blow, and he eked out a pale smile. Just then, police sirens echoed. He saw a flicker of their lights dancing across the walls and people's faces. He took the revolver from his pocket and, raising it weakly, placed the muzzle in his mouth. Pedestrians screamed, but he didn't care. He closed his eyes and pulled the trigger.

His head exploded, launching a large black stain onto the opposite wall as his body fell to the ground. A small stream of blood poured out and drizzled down a gutter. Faces and murmurs gathered around him. A passer-by shook his head in pity, then tossed a page from a newspaper onto the bloodied face. At that moment, the sky began to scatter volcanic ash in grief onto people and the ground.

Chapter 19

Ziad Al-Niqash

January 7

The fifth day

The sun rose, and I was still in my corner on the dirt floor. I was frozen and stone-faced while ants and dung-beetles traversed my body and mosquitoes sucked my blood. I stared into the void. Thoughts wrestled in my head. Suddenly the door opened. Two thin and terrified men wearing once-white underwear entered. The door was then locked. They stayed there, standing in front of the door, their flanks trembling. They quickly looked toward me, then glanced back at the door. I saw death on their faces. Several moments of silence passed before I heard the sound of cars parking outside. One of the two men trembled violently and lost control of his bladder. Urine ran down his leg. He didn't even notice, nor did the other one standing next to him. Suddenly, the room filled with the stench of excrement. The man who had urinated said in a quivering voice:

– Are they going to take us? Are they going to take us?! That's it, right?

The other man, who had the air of a retired physician, didn't answer and just shook his head. The first man burst into tears, then knelt on the ground. The door opened with a huge clang. Three armed men approached. They led the "doctor" outside and the other remained kneeling on the ground. When they saw the faeces on his thigh, they cursed him. One of them came up and beat him on the face with the butt of his rifle. It oozed blood. A voice came from outside, telling them to hurry up. After some hesitation, they grabbed his hands and pulled him along the dirt. He was screaming incoherently and crying as if his breath was nearly used up.

The door slammed shut with a bang. I stood up and walked toward the door, balancing myself against the wall. I listened furtively and heard indistinct voices and murmurs. Stealing a glance through the keyhole, I saw a crowd of men in a line, all standing in their underwear, guarded by masked armed men. Suddenly, I saw one of the armed men make his way toward the door. I jumped to the side. The door opened and, without entering, he tossed clothes and shoes into two piles and locked the door again. I stood there staring, unfazed, at the pile of clothes. I went back to peeking and saw them handcuff the men with plastic zipties, then gruffly loading them into the back of military transport vehicles. Somewhere in the offing, a whistle blew, and the cars departed, a whirlwind of dust trailing behind them. Once the dust settled, I could see outside. It was nothing more than a sprawling dirt field enclosed by high walls and fenced in by barbed wire. Annexes, cars, and gunmen dotted the vast space. I left everything and went back to where I had been sitting and thought about what I had to do. I wondered what I would do! Should I escape? But I was absolutely helpless. Even if I claimed I could, I didn't have the strength for it. A terrible conjunction of impotence and helplessness made the idea of escaping from this camp utter bullshit.

I found myself walking toward the door. I knocked on it forcefully. I waited. The door opened, and a prison guard looked at me. I informed him that I wanted to put my family's mind at ease. He stayed there, staring at me for several seconds, then smiled mockingly and warned me against knocking on the door a second time. I begged him. I told him that my father was ill. He didn't show the slightest concern. He left and slammed the door behind him. I realised that my anxiety and pain meant nothing to these people, and they couldn't give a damn. They—like everyone I had chanced upon, and like everyone this war had produced and supported—were nothing more than savage wolves addicted to blood, made of damnable stone. The darkness of hate and ignorance had long since hollowed out their emotions and capacity for mercy.

The prison guard entered and placed my breakfast on the ground. He told me that the judge would issue his verdict in my case today, and that I needed to prepare to stand trial. I didn't know what he meant by "prepare." However, I got ready mentally to leave my prison and to embrace being able to see and hear anything!

Before noon, the prison guard came over along with three armed men. They blindfolded me with a heavy black bandana and told me that we were going to the judge to hear the verdict. I came out into the sunshine and filled my chest with fresh air. The guard opened the car door and put me in, then sat next to me. The car drove around inside the camp and stopped in front of a two-storey building. They took me out of the vehicle, and the guard gently led me in, giving me the time I needed to make my way with an injured foot. When I arrived in front of the building, the guard patted my back, saying:

– Head upstairs!

I lifted my foot and climbed three steps. He said:

– Walk forward!

I took two steps on the cold tile floor. To my surprise, the fragrance of *oud* filled the space. My prison warden patted me on the back again and said in a low voice:

– To the right.

I turned to the right. I entered a room on the first floor redolent with a mixture of the scent of *oud*, musk, and tea. My escort left me inside and disappeared. An armed man came up and took off my blindfold. I found myself in a spacious room with a few armed men sitting against the wall. At the front of the room, there was a window with a white, diaphanous curtain lowered over it. Sitting behind an expensive red desk was a dignified man in his mid-fifties wearing a military uniform without any insignia. In front of him were a stack of papers, a penholder, and a half-filled glass of tea. I knew then that he was the judge. Next to him were three others wearing military uniforms. I was seated at the back near the door while the judge flipped through the papers in his hands. I called out:

– Your Honour!

An armed man standing next to the door scolded me. The judge raised his eyes from the stack and stared at me from above his thick glasses. I thought he would let me speak, and I got ready to, but one of his aides cut me off, saying in a loud voice:

– We are not about to hear your defence or your excuses. You all are soldiers, and all of you were on the battlefield. We did not take anyone from his home or work.

I interrupted him, casting my eyes about the place looking, for a reason he was addressing me in the plural. I asked him:

– What use is there to trying me in court if you're going to kill me in any case?

The aide whispered something in the judge's ear, and he raised his bushy eyebrows, then placed his large pen beside the papers. He folded his hands on the stack of documents and said in a calm, composed voice:

– We are trying you in court in accordance with what you have said in your statements and what witnesses have testified concerning your activities.

Currently, we are giving your papers one final review in the presence of court clerks, and if we find a loophole, we will use it to help you. We won't hesitate to do so.

The judge continued to thumb through the papers, muttering to his assistants for several more minutes. He jotted down brief observations on one of the papers then bound them up, placing them in a green file. He then interlaced his hands in front of him. He began to recite by heart the verdict of the court. And, after some rhyming and alliteration, he sentenced me to death and fixed the time for after the afternoon prayer.

They returned me to my cell. I was stunned, distressed, and utterly bewildered. I watched for voices and interpreted every movement outside as if it were the summons to implement my death sentence.

Waiting and anticipation exhausted me. I muttered and performed the early afternoon prayer. Then I sat against the wall. I felt an ocean of peace and comfort wash over me. When I finished the late afternoon prayer, I heard a car parking outside. I got up from where I was sitting and waited. The prison guard opened the door. In a state of surrender and defeat, I welcomed him into the room. I asked:

– Has the time come?

He nodded. He came toward me, blindfolded me with a wide headband, and handcuffed my wrists in front with a thick, plastic ziptie. I thought the execution would take place outside the prison. Instantly all my walls collapsed. Real fear inundated me and ripped out my heart. Before we crossed the threshold, I stopped and asked him, trying to push back a lump in my throat:

– Are you going to kill me?

He answered without hesitation:

– Not now.

He stopped talking and then led me toward the Toyota Hilux and helped me get in the back. From an opening in the headband below my eye, I saw a masked, armed man in front of me and another beside me. With us in tow, the vehicle sped off. We left the camp and headed across a bumpy dirt road. The dust choked me. My mind was vacant. Empty. I couldn't believe or fathom that I was within sight of the end. I tried to imagine how I would look as a crumpled corpse on the dirt, how I would receive death. I imagined what a man feels when his soul is torn from him, when his neck is notched, or when the executioner's bullet pierces his skull. Does it hurt? Or is it like waking up from a nap only to find yourself in another world and another life? I would be lying if I said I didn't care. I wanted to cry, to scream, to call out for help. But one thousand and one hands restrained me from doing so. And even if I had, I don't think it would have made a difference in the end.

Only minutes remained now in your hourglass. What would you do with them, you son of a bitch, if you were in my place? There would be many things you would want to do, but there wouldn't be enough minutes or hours or even days. Who exactly do you think is going to give you time to do what you'd like for the very last time in your life? The most merciful among them might give you a swig of water and two minutes to pray, but that's it.

The armed man sitting beside me pulled out a water bottle from his waist and took a drink. I saw on the back of his hand a skull tattoo. I asked him for some water. He didn't respond. I repeated my request. I begged for a sip. He smiled mockingly, then splashed water against my face and put the bottle back in his belt. The armed man sitting next to me roared with laughter. I opened my mouth to the wind and dust. Perhaps it would help me swallow the lump in my throat and extinguish the fire inside it.

The car continued to speed across the rugged dirt path and slope. Numbness welled inside me. Blood trickled from my nose and mouth. I didn't care. Why would I care about that? It would all be shed in moments. The taste of blood surged in my throat. I felt a brush of heat against my chest and stomach. I found myself in a semi-slumber and my life passed before my eyes like a movie. I slumped my head onto my shoulder and assumed the foetal position. After a moment, the vehicle stopped. The driver slapped the door, saying quickly:

– Alright, alright, quickly.

The armed man sitting in front of me got up. He grabbed me by the tail of my shirt and yanked me sharply from my spot. He then threw me out of the vehicle. He got out and held me by the neck and led me away, head lowered. At that moment, I recalled the man I had seen in prison. His bewildered look. How he urinated on himself. I wondered, where is he now? In what state? I wondered whether he was looking down on me from beyond the clouds? Whether he was trying to whisper to me: Don't worry. Everything will end in a second.

We walked a little into the open wilderness. I tripped again and again. The armed man didn't care, but kept pulling me cruelly over the thorns and gravel. In his eyes, I was nothing more than an annoying errand he wanted to dispatch with as soon as possible so he could get on with his life. I prayed to God in my heart. I begged for mercy and forgiveness. I commended my mother and father and sisters to God's protection. A part of the blindfold loosened. The armed man stopped next to a cactus plant, then shoved me forward, saying:

– Walk ahead three steps and lay on your back.

I took three steps and found myself in front of a large pile of dirt. I sat resting against it. He loaded his rifle. All the muscles in my body tightened in preparation for the kill shot. I let out a groan and cried. He approached me quickly, then placed something in my shirt and struck my shoulder with his hand. At that moment, a car horn blared to hurry him up. He looked back and took a few steps. He raised his rifle. I held my breath. He pressed the trigger without hesitation. A sound fired. It wasn't one bullet, but a round of them. Dirt and gravel scattered in my face and my body went limp. The gunmen ran off. My chest filled with the smell of blood and gunpowder.

I heard the car leaving. I didn't feel the least bit of pain in my body. I had heard, in the past, that when a bullet tears through a person's body, it does not cause any pain. I must have been bleeding by now. The whole matter would last only a few minutes and I would depart this world. I praised God that no pain tortured me. Weakness overcame me. A cold wind blew. I closed my eyes and listened to a distant call. I sensed something move over my leg. I opened my eyes to see a lizard. When it felt my movement, it scurried off. It had awakened all my senses. After a few minutes of doubt, I came to the conclusion that I was still alive and that I was able to move my limbs! I took the blindfold off my eyes and felt my body. I didn't find any puncture wound or hole. A few steps away, I saw empty bullet casings. I laughed and cried at the same time. My eyes scanned the barren wasteland. I lifted them toward the sky that had begun at that moment to rain down volcanic ash with a rumble. I kept staring in disbelief and vomited my insides all at once.

Such is the will of God. No one in this world can anticipate His will or workings. I cut the zipties on the side of a sharp boulder. In the distance, I saw an asphalt road and hobbled toward it, without stopping or looking back.

Before darkness fell, I stood panting on the side of the tarmacked road. After some waiting, I saw truck lights coming down the road toward me. I moved forward with every ounce of strength left in my body. I stood in the middle of the road, waving my hands in the face of the oncoming truck. I didn't expect anything, and I had nothing to lose at that moment. Whether

I lived or died, it was all over for me. I had decided that this would be the end, the end of everything. I would accept it however it came.

When only a few metres separated me from the truck, my feet could no longer support me, and my body fell to the asphalt. The truck came to a halt two steps in front of me. The driver leapt out of his seat and made his way toward me with a bottle of water in hand. He stood staring for several moments, then came closer and poured small sips into my mouth. He wiped my neck, then carried me by my armpits toward the truck. He vigorously opened the door, helped me get in, then closed it with a slam. He hurried around the truck to get back in his seat and took off down the road.

Chapter 20

Three Days Later

January 10

3 o'clock in the afternoon

Like a dead man who has forcefully escaped from the grave, I reached the edge of our neighbourhood, weighed down by pain and weakness. My clothes were in tatters and my feet bare. My shoulders hunched. I rested my body on a bowed staff. I was welcomed by an angry knocking sound on an unseen iron gate. I looked all around. All the shops were closed, and all the houses' doors and windows were shut. There was nothing in the streets except for ash, monotony, and the stench of sulphur.

When the knocking stopped, I grasped my stick with a trembling hand and walked on. My feet were submerged in ash. A page from a torn newspaper flew at me, and I pulled it from my face, tossing it aside. From afar, an emaciated dog blanketed in cinders looked at me. He ran up and rubbed against my thigh, letting out a doleful whine. When he grew tired of me, he took off, dragging a trail of whimpers behind him.

I reached our courtyard gate. I stood in front of it, out of breath, exhausted and in pain. I apprehensively touched its iron and decorative metal flowers. On the upper left-hand side of the wall, a laminated poster was hung and covered in ash. I looked at it for several seconds then tapped it with my stick. The ash fell to the ground. I saw myself in a new picture. I was wearing a military uniform in front of a three-coloured flag. At the bottom of the picture, Quranic verses announced my death and stated my name.

I walked away and went back toward the gate. I glanced around the courtyard. Ash was in every crevice and on every branch. The wild camphor tree wasn't standing tall where it had forever, but had turned into a dry, branchless pole that had collapsed, at some point, against the western corner of our house, destroying it. Winter, too, had stripped our grapevine of its leaves. Below it was my father's chair and small table, a heap of ash on both, along with the remnants of leaves and dry branches.

I pushed open the gate. Its rusty joints let out a sharp groan. I tossed my stick aside and walked, balancing on my good foot. My heart began to pound. I saw a pile of women's shoes in various colours and styles at the doorstep of our house. I heard a buzz like the drone of bees. After several steps, the buzzing turned into indistinct muttering. I wasted no time. I pushed the door open and stepped across the threshold.

I was struck by darkness and a wave of warmth, filled with the scent of incense and body odour. Eight eyes fixed on me. Everything went silent, even my breath and the beating of my heart. Moments passed, and then every mouth erupted in cries. Bodies scrambled over each other like a ball of worms. Amid the forest of faces, I saw my mother's, illuminating the darkness and making its way toward me, shouting, completely overcome. My three sisters were behind her weeping, their eyes straining toward me. I spread my hand towards them and tried to smile. But my body collapsed onto the rug and sank into the darkness.

30 October 2019

Bader Ahmed

Author

Five Days Untold is the author's third book. His previous literary works include Black Rain (2013) and Between Two Doors, which was translated into Italian (2019). He resides in Yemen.

Christiaan James

Translator

An American literary translator resident in London. He has lived throughout the Middle East, including Yemen, and holds a degree in Middle East Studies from Harvard University.